EXPEDITION

INTO THE RIFT

EXPEDITION

INTO THE RIFT

JOHN B. HAMMOND

A FINE BOOK INDEED

For information contact:
johnbhammondauthor@gmail.com

Published by:
A Fine Book Indeed

Copy Editors: Barbara Hammond and Audry Hammond
Content Editor: Debra Rasmussen

Cover design by Evan C • 99designs
Interior book design by Francine Platt • Eden Graphics, Inc.

Hardcover ISBN 979-8-89454-001-6
Ebook ISBN 979-8-89454-002-3

Library of Congress Number: Pending

Manufactured in the United States of America

First Edition

Dedicated to

My wonderful wife,
my loving mother,
and my caring sister—
the women who have nurtured
and inspired me.

CHAPTER 1

ALEX WOKE ABRUPTLY.

The driver of the transport looked back at her.

"Apologies, Miss. You would think I'd have learned the potholes by now," he laughed.

Alex was too groggy to appreciate his attempt at humor. Exhausted from a gauntlet of phone calls and paperwork before she left for Switzerland, until now the ride had lulled her tired body to sleep.

It had been almost two years since Alex had left the Air Force. But when a representative of the United Nations approached her about a secret assignment, curiosity dictated her decision.

And secret it was. All she was told was that it would have an impact on global security and that it was a scientific mission. An odd combination.

So, now here she was, barreling up a mountain with two British soldiers.

"I still think there's a better way to do this, Captain," the younger man to her right insisted in a thick accent.

"If you've got suggestions for how to get people up there, I'd be obliged to hear it, Corporal," said the captain.

Both men wore patrol caps, and their uniforms were worn and wrinkled.

The corporal seemed excited. "Alright, hear me out. A ski lift, why not? We're in the Alps! I can't believe no one has thought of this."

The captain bellowed a laugh, "I think I can guess why no one has, Corporal. Once they finish those airship landing pads, we're out of a job. I'd count your blessings while you've still got such an easy assignment, lad."

The odd pair had been bickering about one ridiculous subject after another the entire drive—which was why Alex elected to sleep. They must have done this trip dozens of times to have it down to such a routine.

Their voices faded into the background as Alex watched at least a dozen other vehicles driving up the narrow two-way road. It was a roughly forged pathway of compressed dirt, most likely the result of countless trips by otherwise off-road vehicles.

The smell of the crisp mountain air, mixed with exhaust, was noticeable even from within the vehicle. She wiped the condensation from the small ballistic glass window, visibly scratched from flung gravel and making it hard to see out. The scenery wasn't exactly a sight to behold—a desolate, rocky terrain, with little greenery aside from the few patches of yellowing grass that crept between the rocks. They were at a high altitude, and Alex was grateful to be in a nicely heated, airtight vehicle.

Alex felt something jab her rib and turned to have angry words with the young corporal, only to have her attention stolen by the impressive sight ahead.

To call it a building would be an incomplete statement. It was a tower, but also in some places a bunker, all built at an almost impossible angle into the side of the mountain. It was as if the mountain had swallowed up the skyline of a major city, leaving in view only the tip of the tallest building.

Impressive as it was, it appeared to still be under construction. Scaffolding strutted across the face of the building, and a veritable swarm of cranes lifted and lowered materials. This was the most impressive technical feat Alex had ever seen, even compared to her time in the U.S. Air Force.

"Soon, they'll finish it, and folks won't have to take this dinky little gravel stretch up there," said the captain. "As far as assignments go, it's a pretty amazing place to work, gotta be said."

Alex shook her head, pulling from her stupor, and spoke for the first time since the trip began. "Yeah, I won't argue with that. How long have you two been stationed here?"

"I've been here for five weeks, but the captain has been here since construction began four months ago."

Four months didn't sound right to Alex. Looking at the immense project in front of her, the only way she could think that it was possible to do it so quickly was with the significant cooperation of many countries.

They rolled over a few more small hills, wound across the rough improvised road, entered a long tunnel, and stopped.

A large, almost vault-like door closed behind them, and the surrounding air cycled through. Alex recognized it as an airlock, probably to prevent altitude sickness, rather impressive in this environment.

Emblazoned in white paint on the sealed door was United Nations Anomaly Response Command (UNARC). She had never heard of such an agency, and she wasn't exactly sure what qualified as an 'anomaly'.

Alex looked down the immense tunnel, watching the other vehicles unloading people and crates of cargo. She looked for some sort of clue as to why the base was in such an odd location, why it existed at all, or what it had to do with 'anomalies.' She wasn't able to linger on that thought, interrupted by the creaking of metal as the corporal opened the thick steel door of her transport.

"You doing alright there, Miss? Had a bit of an empty look in your eyes, like you lost where you were," he said.

"Lieutenant, not Miss," she grumbled, "and yeah, sorry, this is a lot to take in."

Alex stepped out of the vehicle, her long legs making it an easier drop than it was for most. At six foot two, Alex towered over the corporal, who barely met her shoulder. In the Air Force, her nickname had been 'Amazon.' It made introductions awkward, especially when she was taller than most of the men in her unit.

As she stood up straight, the corporal looked startled and then intimidated. "Of course, sorry, Lieutenant. Yeah, it can be kinda overwhelming," he rubbed the back of his neck.

"Anyway, I'm heading out with the captain. We've got another group we're bringing up, and the caravan is leaving soon. Nice meeting you, Miss—I mean Lieutenant."

Alex wasn't really listening as she stared down the network of hallways before her, and she paid no mind to his footsteps as he walked away.

This was too much to take in. The massive base, its remote location, the feats of technology all around her, and the chain of events that had led her to all of it. Her mother had always said that it was her adventurous spirit that pulled her into the Air Force.

Alex blamed her parents for that—being an Army brat, she had grown up all around the world. She was sure she broke their poor hearts when she joined the Air Force.

This assignment, with how quickly and secretly it had all happened—none of it felt real. She shook her head, dispelling her disbelief. She decided to focus on the reason for her being here, which she assumed she would soon be told. She expected some sort of guard or attendant to greet her or flag her down, but only scattered workers and people in uniform strolled by. It was like any normal administration building during her time in the military.

This one was, however, built into the side of a mountain. She saw some sort of window off in the distance at the very end of the corridor and cautiously began walking down what she determined to be the central hallway. As she progressed, she passed rooms, common areas, cafeterias, and rows of bunks.

As massive as the building seemed from the outside, Alex quickly determined that it was a lot bigger on the inside. It appeared to stretch deep into the mountain. As she approached the end of the hallway it seemed odd to have a window in a bunker. There was no way to have a view of the outside from here because she was headed deeper into the mountain. When she reached the window she understood.

Beyond the thick glass was a massive cavern, roughly carved out of the stone. Within it was a sprawling set of mundane buildings, out of place, artificial. Past that, an enormous wall separated the buildings from a more open area. She was looking down at a large collection of military vehicles and equipment. From her vantage point in this otherwise mundane hallway, that was all she could see.

As she marveled, someone tapped on her shoulder. Her eyes lingered on the impressive display longer than she intended, but then she turned and came face to face with a large man, barely taller than her, with dark skin and a goofy smile.

"I'm guessing you've had quite the day, Lieutenant Petrakis. I know from experience how boring the drive here can be," he extended his large, muscular hand.

Alex hesitantly accepted the gesture. "I actually slept the whole way."

"Well, that's smart, I wish I had thought of that the first time I got carted up here."

Alex stared blankly. She was used to the formal ceremony affiliated with her line of work, though she didn't like it. The casual demeanor this man presented contrasted the military nature of the assignment. It was odd, almost unnerving.

"Oh, I haven't even introduced myself. I'm Darius," he said. "Sorry I didn't greet you at the gate. Folks are pretty talkative around here, so I tend to run late. Seems you've already started showing yourself around the base, but let's get to the point and show you why you're here."

With that, he swiftly turned around and began walking away at a brisk pace.

Alex was so taken aback at his sudden departure that she had to hurry to catch up.

"Hey! Hang on!" She dashed after him.

People emptied from rooms, flooding the hallway. Squeezing past soldiers and workers, Alex caught up to him. The very moment they entered the crowd, people started greeting the towering man with enthusiasm.

He gave a "Hey" here and a "Morning" there, three waves, two nods, and at least one set of finger guns. Everyone seemed they had somewhere to be, none more so than Darius who was blurring the fine line between walking and jogging. She would have lost sight of him, had they not been the two tallest in the group.

Finally, they squeezed through a pair of elevator doors and halted. Alex bent over, hands on her knees, to catch her breath after the blitz to the elevator. She took a moment to calm herself and stood, finding all eyes on her, something she never enjoyed.

As the elevator descended, she raised a shaky hand in greeting. One person hesitantly waved back.

"Sorry, Alex," said Darius. "Lunch hour. I knew we had to get out of there fast."

She cleared her throat, "Darius, where exactly are we going?"

"To show you the reason you're here."

"How encouragingly vague."

"Most people get restless waiting to see why we're all here, so I like to get it out of the way before anything else. Speaking of…" his voice trailed off as the elevator halted and a beep sounded when the doors opened. There were a few moments of awkward silence before Alex realized she was standing directly in the doorway.

Quickly ducking into a corner, she let the strangers exit, surely having made, in a best-case scenario, an interesting first impression. Darius soon followed, moving at his apparently characteristic fast pace. Less surprised this time, Alex followed quickly after him.

"Isn't there some sort of security screening or something I need to do first? Wow..." Alex paused as she looked around her. She was still in the cave but now on a sidewalk, surrounded by various buildings. The cave ceiling stretched high above her, but there were several independent structures built into the floor. The ground was paved like any normal city. She knew this time to not get side-tracked and quickly focused back on her guide.

As they walked along a road, she watched small vehicles drive up and down the street. It would have been an average, normal town, had it not been sitting underneath millions of tons of mountaintop.

Before she knew it, they arrived at the end of the road and a massive wall. It appeared to her what a barrier to a maximum-security prison might look like, complete with parapets and guards at the top.

Darius flashed a badge at a device on the wall, starting a loud grinding noise. Alex turned her attention to the steel doors as they started to open. They were heavy-duty, possibly nuclear grade. Once the gap was wide enough, Darius proceeded forward, and Alex caught up.

"None of this stuff phases you, does it?" asked Alex.

"Nope, when you've given the tour as many times as I have, it loses its wonder."

On the other side of the wall, there were soldiers from various nations in their respective uniforms manning machine guns, rocket launchers, cameras, sensors, and even a few tanks. All weapons were trained on one point.

That's when she saw what looked like a crack or tear in the air.

It was surrounded by a kind of shimmer, almost like broken glass but smoother, practically liquid. Alex turned to Darius to confirm what she was seeing was real. "What is that?"

Darius gave a knowing grin and looked ahead.

"That," he said, "is the Rift."

CHAPTER 2

ALEX BLINKED REPEATEDLY. There was a major disconnect between what her eyes were seeing and what her brain was willing to believe.

Darius said, "Why don't you come with me and get some answers?"

He opened the flap of a large tent, and Alex hesitantly followed him, but she couldn't stop looking at the Rift.

The tent was dusty and torn in some places, and inside was a makeshift theater with rows of folding chairs and a large screen in front. Alex looked around the nearly empty room and picked a random chair to sit in. Suddenly, the screen lit up.

A presentation began with narration.

"Welcome agents to the *International Suspended Rift Research and Study Installation*. What you've just seen is one of the best-kept secrets of the 21st century. The first documented case of a 'Looking Glass Rift' occurred March 17th, 2056, in the hills surrounding Leeds, England. Two fishermen witnessed it opening in the center of a lake. They posted it on social media and after roundly being mocked, they moved on with their lives.

The information was hidden from the public by the British government, but they later contacted the United Nations. On

August 3, 2056, a Rift opened in the center of a small Austrian military base, and from it emerged large, green-skinned humanoid creatures bearing rudimentary weapons. Despite the initial shock of the attack, the creatures were pushed back into rift with very few casualties to the Austrians.

It was at this point that the *'United Nations Anomaly Response Command'* was formed. The UNARC is a confidential agency of the United Nations dedicated to the study of the Rifts and ultimately the understanding and mitigation of the dangers they pose. All Rifts close shortly after opening, so no science teams could be mustered to their locations with enough time to study them. However, in February 2057 there was a breakthrough."

Alex was still dumbstruck. She looked at Darius for validation. He simply nodded back with that same cheeky smile.

She returned her focus to the presentation, highly engaged.

"A Swiss science team developed a sensor to detect the specific radiation given off by the Rifts. The team planned to plant it on the highest peak they could get to in the Alps, but a storm hit, and they were forced to seek shelter. When they entered a cave, their equipment started detecting radiation. They went deeper into the cave and came upon a larger cavern. Inside was a Looking Glass Rift. They quickly set up their equipment and were able to obtain readings and measurements that no one had been able to get before.

As they studied it, the Rift began to fade and contract, getting smaller and seemed like it would disappear. The team panicked, but just before it was completely gone, it exploded in size, filling the entire cavern.

An arc of electricity was flowing from one of their portable generators, directly into the Rift. The Rift was attracting electricity. They moved more generators close to the Rift, and by upping the voltage, they managed to stop it from contracting.

They contacted the Swiss government, who reached out to the United Nations, and UNARC teams were immediately sent. Sending probes, even cameras through the Rift, proved fruitless. Any electronics that passed through the threshold of the Rift were immediately fried. It was determined that the only way research could be done was by humans. That, agent, is exactly why you're here. You will be part of the first group through the Rift."

Darius stopped the presentation abruptly. "The rest is pretty dull, mostly just a speech about furthering humanity and reaching new frontiers, that sort of thing."

Alex stood, still trying to process everything. "I have…many questions."

Darius smiled, "Construction was started on this place, the Looking Glass, just two weeks after the discovery. Pretty impressive if you think about it, especially given all the bureaucracy involved. It needed to be that quick though. Rifts are opening more and more in recent months. It is only a matter of time before one opens in the middle of a populated area and something comes through." Darius emphasized the last two words in a very dire tone.

Alex was shaken. She hadn't expected these sorts of stakes when she was told this was a scientific mission.

Darius continued, "I'm sorry to say, Alex, but they got you here later than anyone expected. You're going in, now."

"Hold on. Immediately? No training? Just a slideshow and a pep talk?"

Darius nodded. "That presentation is a bit outdated, when the research team found the Rift they could see through it to the other side. It was some sort of grassy field. Over time though, a space between our side and the other side formed. It used to be you could have just stepped through it, but now the void is almost two-hundred feet. It's getting farther each and every day. Our science team thinks it has something to do with the electricity we're pumping into it. They pump just enough to keep it open; they say it's destabilizing it. But if we don't, the gap could totally close. Seems someone higher-up thought you'd be fine for the job without any training."

They exited the tent and Alex pondered why she had been picked. True, she had a fairly impressive record, but she wasn't particularly prominent. She didn't stand out in any way that she knew of.

The closer they got to the Rift, more and more weapons and soldiers came into view. Clearly, if anything with ill intent were to come through the Rift, it would be met with considerable force. Cables, tents, and small pop-up buildings covered the area. Had she not known she was in a massive cavern, Alex would have felt like she was back at any average military camp.

Darius gestured to a small loosely assembled group. "Come meet your team."

The first was a small but stocky woman with fiery red hair tied up into a tight bun. Sparks flew from a small instrument wrapped around her wrist as she tinkered with it. She turned her attention to Alex and crossed her arms. She seemed self-assured and, after briefly looking Alex up and down, nodded and went back to working on her equipment.

"This is Charlotte Sharot. Your technology expert. She'll be handling all of your equipment and gadgetry," Darius explained.

The woman waved a hand over her shoulder and without looking away from her work said, "I go by Charlie."

"Next up is Isaac Ross. He'll be in charge of logistics and supply."

A thin man with short black hair stood at attention and awkwardly saluted Darius.

"Yes, hello sir, hello ma'am!"

Darius pinched the bridge of his nose. "Isaac, we talked about this. You don't need to salute anyone here. This isn't the military."

"Sorry sir, I mean Darius. It's just a force of habit." He turned to Alex, "Nice to meet you Miss—what's your name actually?"

"Alex."

"Nice to meet you, Alex. Wow, you're tall, I wish I was that tall. I'm pretty short for my family…"

As Isaac rambled, Alex turned to Darius and whispered, "Is this really what he's like?" Darius nodded with a grin.

Isaac continued, "But yeah, my brothers always teased me about my height,"

"Right," She looked at the younger man who couldn't be any older than twenty and began to wonder how any of them had ended up here. She moved on to the final team members. A man and a woman, they fiddled with each other's equipment and bickered quietly.

"No, I take this, you take that."

"I know what I'm doing Alicia, we have to hurry up, they're gonna be here soon."

Darius cleared his throat, louder than he needed to.

The two turned suddenly, in uncanny unison.

"Hello!" The woman beamed, "I'm Alicia and this is Anthony."

The man waved halfheartedly.

Darius interjected, "Anthony will be your science specialist and Alicia will handle recording and documenting everything you see on the other side. She's also a linguistic specialist."

The pair perplexed Alex. Both were the same height and had the same brown hair. They seemed like mirror images of one another save eye color and well, gender.

"Are you two twins?"

"Actually…"

Alicia interrupted Anthony. "Oh, we get that all the time. We're dating."

"But not twins who are dating, because that would be really weird," Anthony finished. Their way of speaking was bizarre, not each on their own, but as they spoke their speech was interwoven like it was being spoken by a single person. They literally finished each other's sentences.

"Well, I'll let you get back to your equipment," said Alex, escaping the conversation.

She walked away from the group and began speaking to Darius out of their earshot. "I now have very many questions. I didn't sign up to go into another dimension or whatever. Especially with only a handful of people, only half of which can even fight."

Alex was losing her composure. It was all too surreal, and she felt tricked into this bizarre situation.

Darius shrugged, "The higher-ups figured a smaller team would be better, and if there were any sort of political entity on the other side, they would see a large military force as an invasion. We'll be going in, taking some readings, and reporting back."

"We?" Alex shot back.

"I'm your final team member, Darius Byron. I'll be your security detail."

"Thanks, but I can handle myself."

"Hey, I'm sure you can. I'm there for the others. Although you'd be surprised, they can handle themselves pretty well too. Charlie is a technician for the FBI. Isaac was in the Army. Anthony and Alicia are both CIA analysts."

Alex sighed and looked back over at the group, now all lined up with their vests fitted and equipment stowed, ready to go. "This is…a lot."

Darius' grin disappeared, and he looked directly at her. "Listen,

Alex, I don't know why you were picked, but frankly speaking, if you were selected for something this important, I figure a lot of smart people believe you can do this. These people need someone, this is gonna be the most important assignment of their lives. They need a leader."

Alex looked into Darius' brown eyes and watched as the grin returned to his face, this time a hint of encouragement lying behind it. She looked at the Rift, then at her new team, and took a deep breath.

Gathering her resolve, she turned back to Darius. "Is there anything else you can tell me about the mission that wasn't in that silly slideshow?"

"Only a few things. All of your electronic equipment will be stowed in a shielded container. There's no gravity in the Rift, but there is an atmosphere inside, and we've determined that it's breathable to humans. You'll be carrying a cable with you that we'll use to anchor down on the other side. Hopefully, we'll be able to send supplies along the cable. You've got some base tactical equipment on your vests, a sidearm, and camping equipment in the off chance that it closes while you're on the other side."

"That is more than a few things."

"Not when you consider how many unknowns there are on the other side. There is one human that's come through."

Alex stopped him, "What?"

"Here, they've provided you with a brief list of words that we've determined from his language. They call him Mister John Doe."

Darius handed Alex a small handbook. She flipped through and found very little of it relevant. Some words like cow and ocean didn't seem like they'd come in handy, but home and monster might. There were pictures along with the words. Each word was written in both English, a strange runic script that Alex assumed was the language from the other side of the Rift, and an English-style pronunciation for each of the other words. Alex tucked the book into her pocket.

Darius excused himself to brief the rest of the team while Alex began to prepare her own equipment.

She emerged from the changing booth, now dressed in dark gray cargo pants, a similarly hued tactical sweater with long sleeves and a light bulletproof vest. All of her team were similarly dressed, and altogether it looked less and less like a research expedition and more like a SWAT team, which Alex certainly preferred to wearing a lab coat. She walked over to the equipment table and suddenly felt much more in her element.

She recognized a great deal of it from her time in the military, but all of it seemed much more cutting edge than a federal budget could typically afford. A radio, a wrist-mounted touchscreen computer, and a host of armor pads.

But the most interesting to Alex were the weapons they had been provided with. The M186 was the standard for most police officers, not some sort of military force, a 3-in-1 Pistol/Stun-Gun/Shell combo that many just called the 'triple threat.' It was a bulky weapon to have in a holster, but the ability to choose between lethal and non-lethal seemed to make up for that. The gear, the equipment, the weapons, this was Alex's element.

She wasn't the best with people, especially new people. She supposed that would have to change, and quickly, if she was going to lead this team. Despite Darius' speech earlier, she was still apprehensive about being in this position. She was also deep down a bit excited. She joined the Air Force to see the world, and this was leagues beyond that promise of adventure.

She tightened up her vest and left the rest of the equipment to be loaded into the shielded container. She walked over to her team and was actually impressed at how professional they looked. Their previously cluttered tables had all been cleared of gear, no doubt taken to the container that would follow them into the Rift. All they had on them were their own vests, some basic non-electronic equipment, and their apparent willingness to go quite literally into the unknown.

The team looked at her expectantly, and she took a deep breath. "Listen, guys. I'm not the best at this. If I was some sort of big-shot military captain or some such, I'd be giving you a big rousing speech to get you motivated. But honestly, you all know that what we're about to do is dangerous, borderline crazy. We've only just met, and I can't speak to your own personal reasons for being willing to do this, but I just want to say that whatever your purpose here is, I already respect you for stepping up. Let's head out." She feigned confidence as she walked towards the shimmering tear in space.

The closer she got, she noticed more soldiers and weapons aimed at the Rift. There was a large Tesla coil behind the rift, pumping an arc of electricity directly into it. A scientist in a plain white lab coat walked up to the group and began instructing them in a thick Eastern-European accent.

"Hello, I'm Dr. Romanov. Each of you will take one of these," she said as each team member was handed a strange device that looked like one of those little sea scooters used by scuba divers. "Each of these has a series of gimbaled RCS thrusters. This is the same technology used on spacecraft to maneuver in zero gravity. They have very little fuel, so please use them sparingly. Try to drift on your own momentum as much as you can, only using these to correct your trajectory. Does everyone understand?"

A series of nods acknowledged the instructions, and each team member began looking over the strange and bulky machines.

A guard gestured to a thick set of cables with a carabiner clip on the end. "Miss Petrakis, you'll have this hooked onto your vest. It will be used to establish an anchor on the other side."

The same scientist continued, "The container with your equipment will be weightless once it passes the threshold. We'll give it initial momentum with these rails, but two of you will have to hold on to it and guide it into the Rift on the other side using your RCS rigs."

Alicia quickly raised her hand, volunteering herself and Anthony. Everyone walked over to the large, shielded container. A pale dark green color, it looked like any standard shipping container. It was on a set of rails, with a battering ram looking device ready to slam into the back of it and push it into the rift.

Alicia and Anthony gripped either side of it, and the rest of the team positioned in front of it.

The Rift was much smaller than the container, so Alex was perplexed as to how they were getting it in.

Dr. Romanov called over the radio, "Power up the reactors." Suddenly the Tesla coil glowed bright red with energy and the arc of electricity spilling into the Rift grew in intensity. The Rift began to slowly expand, stopping after a few moments at a size that would comfortably fit the container.

"You'll want to get a running start, good luck out there," Dr. Romanov told Alex before backing away. "Cut the power."

The arc from the coil suddenly disappeared, and the coil began to return to its normal metallic sheen as it cooled off.

Alex took a deep breath and looked into the Rift. A tiny dot of light framed by the darkest black she had ever seen. She closed her eyes, breathed out and shouted, "Go, go go!"

CHAPTER 3

It was a bizarre feeling. Alex had expected some sort of resistance as she entered, like diving into a pool of water, but instead, it felt like the ground beneath her just gave way. She drifted away from the only source of light, turning around to see where she had entered. Through the shrinking Rift she could see all the personnel on the other side—guards, soldiers, researchers. Also prevalent at this point were about 200 guns of various sizes pointed directly at her. A chill ran down her spine, and she quickly redirected her attention back to her team, who were silently drifting around her. That was one of the strangest things, the complete lack of sound.

It was maddeningly silent; she could only hear the breathing of her teammates along with the occasional rustle of their clothing. In fact, each of her senses were wildly deprived here. The only scent she could smell was that of her own clothing, and the metal of her weapon she had brought with her into this sterile environment. She was sure that spending too much time in this negative space would drive her insane. She was getting claustrophobic, something she had never experienced before.

Charlotte was already prepping her RCS rig, the manually pumped device spurting out a pale white foam. Alex watched her struggle to get a handle on it, but Charlotte quickly stabilized herself into a steady drift without any rotation.

Isaac was having the time of his life, the only thing stopping his sheer amazement was the stray foam from Charlotte, trying to maneuver her RCS, hitting him square in the face.

Alex turned her attention to her own machine. Compared to all the high-tech, cutting-edge equipment they had been issued today; the analog device seemed practically ancient. It was roughly the shape of an egg, with protruding nozzles in every direction. Two handles like a bicycle jutted out from the top. It was anything but ergonomic. It had a lever in the center, going in four different directions. The lever had a twist to it as well, probably adding up to six degrees of movement. A small valve wheel on the side seemed to control the pressure. Taking note of all this, and being a trained pilot, it was fairly easy for Alex to begin adjusting her trajectory with small puffs from the strange contraption.

No sooner had she lined herself up with the literal light at the end of the tunnel, she heard a scream from behind her. She turned her head to see Isaac rotating rapidly; he clearly did not understand the joystick twisted left and right. The momentum of the spin flung him off of the machine, sending him and the machine in opposite directions. Luckily, Isaac was going straight towards the exit—almost. He drifted up and to the right, completely unable to affect his own travel at this point.

Alex was prepared to use what little fuel she had to jet over to him, but before she could, Charlotte adeptly adjusted her direction of travel to meet Isaac. She floated over to him, grabbed the spinning man, and latched him to her. At the same time, she countered their rotation with the device.

Alex was impressed. Charlotte was a quick learner. They lined back up with the exit, and Alex took one last look back where they had come from. It was now a tiny pin prick of light. She figured they must now be dead in the center.

It was dark.

The container had now eclipsed the light from where they entered.

Alex grabbed a glow stick from one of her vest pouches and snapped it. It immediately lit the area around her.

The others followed suit, and a series of cracks filled the silence. She could see her team again, this time in a dizzying array of colors. It seemed each member of the team had a different color, some sort of organizational tool, she supposed.

The exit began to grow in size as they approached it. No longer a pinprick, she could see the bright light. Her eyes had adjusted to the pitch darkness, and now as they approached the end of this seemingly endless corridor of black, the light was blinding. All she could really see was the shimmer of the rift, and the pure brilliant whiteness inside of that shimmer.

Alex steadied her grip on the RCS, taking a moment to fine tune her movement and line up perfectly with the exit. She glanced over her shoulder at the rest of her team: Isaac clinging to Charlotte for dear life, Alicia and Anthony gripping tightly to the sides of the container, moving slower behind everyone else.

Darius had slowed down to match the speed of the rest of the group, and Alex was now in the lead. She looked straight ahead, took in another deep breath, and prepared to enter the unknown.

The bizarre feeling from when she entered returned, this time in reverse. For a brief moment, she felt gravity in front of her, while the rest was weightless, and she popped out the other side like a kid coming down a water slide on their belly. She had let go of the RCS, not wanting it to drag her down with its considerable weight. She rolled, head over heels, down a slight slope. She heard the others land near her, Isaac, and Charlotte noticeably off course. Alex had only a moment to glance around her, seeing a vast sea of green, before she remembered the container.

"Everyone out of the way!" she dived to the side just as the large metal box came sliding past her, momentum carrying it past them.

As the dust settled and the container came to a halt, Alex took a quick survey of her team. Darius was already standing, dusting himself off. Charlotte was shoving the still clinging Isaac off of her and Alicia was walking over to check on a visibly shaken Anthony. Her worries alleviated for the moment; Alex returned to their new surroundings.

It was just an open field of tall, deep green grass. On the horizon she could see a ring of trees surrounding the Rift. Alex didn't know exactly what she was expecting, some sort of alien landscape at least, but this was remarkably—normal.

She heard a clunk and turned to see Charlotte opening the container. The large doors swung open, revealing a walk-in closet style equipment cache. Anthony and Alicia retrieved the scientific equipment for readings and recordings. Darius stepped in next, handing out weapons to each person, and then taking his own.

Alex grabbed her own gear and continued to inspect the surrounding area. She couldn't get over it. It looked so completely average. Like some random field in the middle of midwestern America. The sky was the same shade of blue, the clouds the same shapes, the only oddity was the way they got here. It was at this moment Alex remembered the cable.

She detached the carabiner from her vest, and it fell limply to the ground. The segment still in the rift remained weightless. Darius handed her a stake from the container, and she drove it deep into the ground with a mallet. They now had an anchor between worlds, so that was pretty neat she guessed, as unimpressive as it looked.

Charlotte began setting up a pulley system and Alex went to check on Isaac.

"You doing alright, Isaac? That must have been pretty intense."

Isaac was still catching his breath, "Yeah, no, it was, that was kinda nuts. Wish they had given us more training on all of this before just tossing us in, although I understand the time crunch."

Alex held out a hand and helped Isaac up.

"What's next boss?" he said.

"We let the lovebirds over there get their data and send it back through the Rift, as far as I can tell. Then we wait for further orders," Alex looked over her shoulder. "Hey, you two, what's the situation with you and your science stuff? Are we good to send the data back?"

Anthony was staring at a tablet he held in his hands with Alicia looking over his shoulder, equally invested in its display.

"Guys? Are you getting something weird or exciting over there?" called Alex again.

The pair broke from their daze.

Anthony spoke first, "Y-yeah, it's just these readings…"

"They're...remarkably normal," Alicia finished.

Alex's eyes narrowed, "Normal? Like what?"

"Like Earth normal," Anthony continued. "The only differences here against a baseline of Earth in terms of atmosphere is a lack of pollution, and a slightly higher percentage of oxygen in the air."

"And the gravity is identical to earth, down to the decimal," said Alicia.

"Are you saying we're on Earth?" asked Alex.

"No. No N-no no no!" the two stammered.

"The constellations are different, we're very much on a different planet," Anthony clarified. "It's just . . . almost everything is Earth-like. This is a very normal seeming alien world."

Alex pondered for a moment, wondering what this all meant before dismissing it. This was their field, not hers.

"Well, whatever your readings are, get 'em set up to send back over."

"Yes, Ma'am." Alicia's eyes were still glued to the tablet screen.

Alex rolled her eyes and turned back to Darius, who was inspecting his weapon.

"You think we'll actually have to use those, Darius?"

"Ma'am, there could be anything from bears to aliens to a full-on army out there. If they'd have let me, I would have brought a *tank* through the Rift."

"You know how to drive a tank?"

"Well, no, but you know what I mean. I'll take anything I can get to defend against whatever crazy stuff is over here."

"Fair point."

Some time passed before Anthony gave the thumbs up, and they sent a smaller shielded box with all the data back through the rift on the pulley that Charlotte had hooked up to the cable and anchor.

Darius, laid down in the thick grass, just soaking in the sunlight. He exhaled, loudly and deliberately, and said, "This is by far the freshest air I've ever breathed. This place is amazing. It's like it's completely untouched."

Alex gave him a halfhearted and somewhat forced smile, clearly unable to match the large man's sheer positivity.

A few more minutes passed before the squeaking sound of the pulley could be heard once again. Charlotte hoisted up the container, filled with new drives for more data collection and an envelope with *'Petrakis'* written in fine handwriting on the front.

"Oh, they sent us a letter." Alex flipped open her pocket knife and slit the envelope. Inside was only a flash drive, which Alex quickly plugged into her wrist-mounted computer. The drive contained a lengthy collection of text documents, a PDF of the language handbook, and front and center, a document labeled *'Read first.'*

Alex followed the document's advice and opened it first thing.

Greetings, Agent Petrakis. Congratulations on your successful first journey into the Rift. The report from Agent Daniels indicates you are all in good health. The analysis of your collected data is ongoing, but the first conclusions our people have made are that you are on an earth-like planet with a breathable atmosphere and no lethal radiation. Operating under these assumptions, your orders are simple.

Alex squinted and then blinked.

Isaac piped up. He seemed nervous at her silence since opening the letter. “What does it say? What are our orders?”

Alex continued to examine the letter to make sure she wasn’t missing anything.

“It just says *explore*.”

CHAPTER 4

"THEY SERIOUSLY couldn't give us anything better than *explore?*" Charlotte groaned from behind.

Alex stopped walking, pinched the bridge of her nose, and turned around. "Like I said, Charlotte, the text documents had instructions for *every* conceivable contingency. Direct combat, alien contact, and biohazard, but apparently no one who makes decisions in the entirety of the UNARC ever stopped to think that we'd find a completely normal empty field. They need more info than just *'everything is fine'* so we're gonna go get it and report back once we *have* said info."

"I heard you. I'm just saying it's stupid. Sounds like you agree," Charlotte shot back.

"It's stupid, yes, but I understand the thinking behind it."

Alex continued her march. It had been nearly an hour since they had left the Rift. They had locked their valuable equipment back in the container, hoping that the heavy shielding would keep any possible would-be thieves from getting in. Now they were here, walking through a dense forest in the general direction of west, with no particular destination in mind. Wandering aimlessly on foot through the middle of nowhere carrying heavy gear was what Alex wanted to avoid when she decided to join the Air Force, and yet here she was.

Despite disliking her situation, her surroundings were another story. They were now trudging through a dense forest of oak, or what looked like oak trees, but appeared to be completely untouched.

The light filtering through the gaps between the leaves of a dense tree cover was beautiful, and apart from the sounds of their own marching it was quiet, still, and serene. The dense overgrowth did make walking rather difficult, most of them nearly tripping at some point and constantly getting their packs stuck on low-hanging branches.

Eventually, they decided to stop and set up camp. Alex took this opportunity to read up on the text documents included with the flash-drive.

> When the UNARC began to research the Rift incidents and what they had in common, it was determined that the creatures and monsters were all coming from the same place, another world, planet, or dimension. Theories ranged widely, from aliens to time travel, but eventually some cases of strange humans coming through were seen. One thing was established as consistent: at all the locations this occurred, witnesses saw the same 'crack' in the air. A tear in reality, the sort calculated in theory for decades, but otherwise relegated to the realms of science fiction. A portal or a gateway, eventually the term 'Rift' became the standard. The only common pattern was their visual description, otherwise nothing was known about them. They would appear at entirely random times and locations, and then disappear shortly afterwards. In some cases, people claimed they had known people who went through the Rifts but never came back, and often something came from the other side. The range of creatures was vast, from a human seemingly out of another time period to one incident with what could only

> be described as a dragon. It was noted that the 'visitors' sometimes seemed to align closely with the mythological legends of whatever region they appeared in. The rapidly prevailing theory was that the folktales and legends from around the world were the products of past encounters with these rifts.

By the time Alex stopped reading, the only thing illuminating their campsite was the blazing fire. She could catch only brief glimpses of the stars through the cracks in the forest cover, and whatever light the moon gave off was not strong enough to pierce the treetops.

Alex sat, cross-legged, in her tent. She had been doing her reading on her wrist computer, but now she took it off. They were interesting devices; they had an earlier model back in the Air Force. A curved, flexible screen that wrapped around the arm, like a bendy tablet. It functioned essentially as any smartphone but was much easier to use and keep track of in dangerous situations.

Alex peered around the camp.

Darius was fully unconscious; he had been like that since a few minutes after they all settled down for the night. His snoring was loud, but not unbearable, although Alex wondered if she'd feel the same if they were sharing a tent.

Alicia and Anthony's tents were opposite one another, and each lay on their stomachs, facing each other and discussing their various scientific findings. Charlotte's tent was the only one zipped closed, although she had a dim light on.

Curiously, Isaac had his sleeping bag slightly outside of the tent, so his head was poking out.

"Isaac," she whispered.

He looked up at her.

"Why do you have your sleeping bag like that?"

"The stars," he said, pointing straight up.

Alex leaned out of her tent and, sure enough, above Isaac was a large gap in the tree cover where the stars could be seen clearly. Isaac's gaze returned to the sky.

Alex watched him noting the simple joy in his expression, or was it his eyes? Something about his face was joyful, content. Alex had always enjoyed watching people in these quiet moments, the genuine ones, where she felt she could understand others best.

That thought hung with her as she leaned back into her tent. She really didn't know any of these people. So far they had seemed to all be competent in their technical abilities, but personally speaking they were complete strangers that she had to trust, and who had all been instructed to trust her. She was still grappling with that concept, being a leader. It wasn't the responsibility that scared her, she had dealt with that before. It was the attention, that's what really got her. It was hard to keep a low-profile and just work when you were the person everyone turned to. It hadn't happened much yet, but she knew that one day's worth of leading wasn't long enough to make any judgements. So far though, everyone worked well together, and had been pretty independent. Maybe she had just gotten lucky.

Maybe they were just as Darius said, highly skilled professionals who didn't *need* much direction or training.

"Hey boss," Isaac whispered, interrupting Alex's thoughts. "Why are *you* still awake?"

Alex looked at Isaac, and then at her wrist computer, "Reading up on the whole Rift thing mainly, it's a lot to take in so quickly isn't it?"

"I guess, I wouldn't know. I've been here a few weeks, so I got it in more bits and pieces."

Alex had forgotten that she was the last person on the team who had made it to the Looking Glass. Darius had said something about her being later than expected, hence the rush to get them all through the Rift itself.

"Oh right. I guess I was late to the party so to speak, what about the others?"

Isaac sat up in his sleeping bag, "I only met Charlie yesterday at lunch, but she said she's been there a few weeks."

Alex wondered about Charlotte, she had spoken very little since they had met, only really piping up to correct someone or disagree with something.

"Alicia and Anthony have apparently been with the science folks at the UNARC since before construction even started on the base."

Those two hadn't been apart the whole time they had been here. Alex was surprised they had separate tents at all.

"Not sure about Darius, he was always here as far as I can tell, everyone on base seems to know him."

Darius seemed to be a genuinely nice person, and he also seemed to know what he was doing more so than anyone in the group.

"What about you, boss? How'd you end up on this mission?" asked Isaac.

Alex was a bit taken aback; she hadn't expected such a direct question from Isaac.

"Oh, well I used to fly for the Air Force. I retired, but the whole 'secret assignment from the United Nations' thing was intriguing enough for me to bite I guess."

"Oh cool, I was in the Army, combat engineering and logistics stuff ya know? One day my boss comes to me and says I can either get stationed back in the states or go get a security clearance and work some secret job in Switzerland. I didn't want to go home, and I'd never seen the Alps before, so I figured it was a good plan."

"Didn't want to go home?"

"Oh gosh, I didn't mean to make it sound dire. It's not like there are any problems there or something, but I joined the army to see the world. See exciting new places and people, kinda hard to do that in Nebraska."

Alex smiled, “You must have been pretty excited to go through the Rift then, that’s a lot more exotic than Switzerland.”

“Oh. I couldn’t wait! I wasn’t originally here to do the Rift jump, just helped with the construction of the Looking Glass. When they decided the American team was going through first though, I was on a short list of logistics experts. Just lucked out I guess.”

Alex was relaxed, probably for the first time since she had gotten to Europe. She hadn’t expected a casual fireside conversation, but apparently it was just what she needed. She was finally getting tired, and a yawn escaped her. “Well, I’m glad to have you on the team, Isaac. We should probably both sleep, there’s no telling what we’ll be in for tomorrow.”

Isaac nodded and laid back down.

As Alex zipped up her tent, she saw Isaac’s eyes, however tired, turned back to the stars.

CHAPTER 5

THE NEXT MORNING, it didn't take long to make it out of the trees. As the sunlight returned, they saw ahead of them a massive hill, topped with bright green grass. Alex opted for them to go to the top to gain a higher viewpoint and figure out a destination; if they were lucky enough to find one.

Once they reached the top, Alex took off her heavy pack, dropped it on the ground and sat next to it. After a few minutes, she noticed Isaac scanning the horizon with some binoculars.

"Uh, boss I think I've found something," he didn't look away from his discovery.

"What is it?" Alex was still slightly out of breath.

"It looks like a village," Isaac sounded uncertain.

"You mean like a town?"

"No, literally a village. Like, old-school, medieval times *village.*"

Isaac was lying prone on the grass. Alex crawled over to him and took the binoculars. It took her a moment to find it, but through the lenses she could see stone houses, thatched roofs, and fields of cattle.

She sighed, "Huh, alright that's unexpected thing number five for this week."

"Ma'am if you don't mind, I have a theory," said Isaac.

"Shoot."

Isaac continued, "A lot of the monsters that came through the portals were consistent with mythology and fantasy from around the world right? What if the technology level of the people living in *this* world is similar to when those myths were written?"

Alex raised her eyebrows, "You're saying that there are knights and peasants running around?"

"I mean we already know there are dragons, knights sort of go hand-in-hand with them in the stories," said Charlotte, having appeared seemingly out of nowhere on Isaac's other side.

"Exactly!" Isaac beamed.

"I've got to be honest; I'm concerned by how much your theory *does* makes sense, Isaac." Alex groaned. "The language handbook they gave us doesn't have words for stuff like car or phone, things we have in the modern world."

"Well, on the bright side that means no super advanced aliens are gonna zap us with lasers. If we get in a fight, the other side will have *swords,* so I'd say we'll be alright," said Charlotte.

"Yeah, that's assuming all of our fights start outside of *sword* range," Alex chided.

"Fair enough," said Charlotte. "But still, I like our odds."

Alex stood and brushed the dust off her pants. "Well let's try to avoid it either way," I know one thing, if we walked into an actual medieval town dressed like a SWAT team, we'd stick out pretty bad."

She started to undo the clasps of her vest, removed her bulky armor, followed by her sweater, leaving only her T-shirt and pants.

She looked around, "I don't suppose any of you packed a cloak or something similarly old-fashioned?"

"Raincoats, but those are nylon." Darius looked curiously at Alex, "Are you planning on going in there?"

He seemed concerned as well as curious.

"Well, if our mission is to gather information, I think asking around is better than continuing to wander aimlessly through the woods, don't you?"

"Doesn't it seem a bit dangerous? If they see us as outsiders, they could get hostile," said Darius.

"Considering what we are prepared for, I'd say this is a lot less dangerous than expected," said Alex.

"You're the boss. What's the plan then?"

"Isaac and I will head down in whatever disguises we can throw together, the rest of you stay up here. Darius, I want you pulling security and Charlotte—"

"Charlie."

"Charlie will keep watch on us from the hill. Do you have binoculars?"

Charlie surprised Alex when her face lit up.

"Better! I've got my baby!" Charlie hurriedly opened a large pocket in her bag. She pulled out a folded rifle, and with a flick she extended it to a full-length sniper-type rifle. It appeared to fire a *very* large bullet.

Charlie beamed as she displayed it for them. "My own model 25-millimeter specialized payload rifle. I've got a dozen different ammunition types of a wide variety, and the best optics you could ask for. AI enhanced multi-spectral imaging, twenty-five times zoom, and a ballistics computer." She practically hugged the weapon.

Alex was beginning to get a better idea of Charlie's personality, now that she had spoken more than five words. Clearly she too, was more comfortable with her own interests.

"Sounds good," Alex smiled, happy to have a better understanding of her teammate.

Minutes later, both Isaac and Alex were dressed in pale green raincoats, the hoods pulled over their heads, and carrying what little equipment they could fit in the pockets of their cargo pants.

The notable exception was the inclusion of a bulky holster for their pistols that they each wore on the back of their waist to be out of sight. It was an awkward setup, but from the outside they both looked like mysterious travelers out of a fantasy story, albeit with pants that may stick out due to the sheer number of pockets.

Alex sighed, "Well, that's probably as close as we're gonna get for now." Out of the corner of her eye she could see Isaac fidgeting, and when she turned to look at him he quickly looked away.

"Is something wrong, Mister Ross?" asked Alex.

"Well Ma'am it's just that—well you're a woman," said Isaac sheepishly.

Alex raised an eyebrow, perplexed by the obvious statement. "So, I've been told, is there a problem with that?"

"Well, if we really *are* in some sort of medieval or fantasy style setting, wouldn't you be wearing a dress or something?" Isaac was visibly losing confidence with every word that escaped his mouth.

Charlie failed to stifle a chuckle.

Alex stared at him, the confused and now somewhat angry look remained on her face.

"Isaac I'm going to let you mull over how stupid that question was."

"Y-Yes Ma'am."

CHAPTER 6

WHEN THEY ENTERED THE TOWN, the streets were crowded with people dressed in an appropriate manner for a medieval time period.

Alex couldn't help but think back to stories she had read as a kid. This place reminded her of a fairytale or fantasy novel. She had never *disliked* those stories, but she hadn't been particularly infatuated with them either.

The farther they went into the village, the smell of campfires and strange spices dominated Alex's senses. They had come through some sort of market square, and it soon became apparent that the surrounding trees had made this town seem smaller than it actually was.

While it certainly wasn't a city, or even comparable to a decent sized town back on Earth, for its era it seemed fairly extensive. Wooden carts and booths lined either end of the cobblestone road, and people shopped and haggled all around them.

The town appeared to be decorated with banners and lines of small flags strung between buildings. They seemed new and were perhaps part of some event or celebration. That would also explain the atmosphere, unless this was the happiest town on this planet, and it was like this every day.

Entertainers drew the attention of small children, and music increasingly filled the air as they approached the center of town. Alex was somewhat relieved, it would be easier to go unseen in a crowd, although she never enjoyed large gatherings of people back home.

Alex looked around at the villagers, attempting to remain discreet. The choices they had made for their disguises were not terribly off, if a bit nicer and more utilitarian than most of the outfits found in the square.

Isaac's eyes were shining, like a kid in a candy store.

"You alright there, Isaac?" she asked.

"Yeah, it's just that this is like every beginning town in every RPG, ever."

Alex knew enough about video games to know what he was referring to, and while it had not occurred to her up to that point, it did remind her of a game she played when she was very young.

"Well, you're not wrong," Alex kept her eyes forward.

After walking for a bit, they met a fork in the road. Alex turned to Isaac, "Remember, try to blend in." She looked around, he was nowhere to be seen.

She retraced her steps. At least the disguises worked.

Alex closed her eyes and took in a deep breath to calm down, she isolated the sounds in her head and filtered out the crowd, listening for a clue. As with any active crowd the primary sound was that of shuffling feet, followed closely by a multitude of disparate voices, all speaking a language (or languages, she couldn't tell) that she didn't understand. After a few moments though, she heard a distinctly English word.

"Amazing!"

Alex moved toward Isaac's voice and found him admiring a finely decorated sword on a pedestal. She looked past the display to see what was clearly an old-school blacksmith shoppe. The burly, sweating man by the fire hammered out another sword right then and there.

Isaac was practically drooling over what appeared to be an antique weapon.

She noticed only at the last moment as Isaac's outstretched hand drifted towards the sword, but before she could react, the angry blacksmith shouted, "Gorto! Thu'resh, thu'resh!"

He shooed Isaac away from the evidently valuable piece. The bearded man continued, speaking incomprehensibly fast what she assumed was some sort of terse warning directed squarely at Isaac.

It was all gibberish to Alex.

She had skimmed through the very limited language handbook they had been provided with, but none of it stuck, certainly not in the short time she'd had to read it. Nonetheless she took it from her pocket and searched.

The words were mostly nouns. Things, animals, and landscapes dominated the list, with concepts and conversational language scant at best. Eventually, Alex came to a word that was listed in English as *sorry*—Tignaucht.

"Tignaucht! Tignaucht." She varied her pronunciation slightly to get a feel for the word. However poor her speech, it had clearly gotten across to the blacksmith, who seemed to relax.

His previously angry demeanor was now one of friendly curiosity, and he began to study the two strangers in front of him.

"Ko...Pah'moth, chayiv'to?" he said, Alex noted his inflection and his raised brow, and deemed it a question. A quick flick through the book yielded nothing but *chayiv'to* being translated as yes and/or correct.

"What?"

The word didn't seem to mean anything to the man, but her look of sheer confusion certainly made an impression.

He repeated his question, slower and enunciating certain syllables. "*Pah'moth...*chayiv'to?" The first word was accompanied by a finger pointed at both Isaac and Alex, whereas the second remained in a question tone.

Alex concluded he was asking them if they were *something*. Whether he was asking if they were new in town or asking if they were thieves was beyond her, but the tone of his question had seemed friendly, so Alex replied with a very cautious affirmation of "Chayiv'to?"

The blacksmith grinned and began speaking rapidly again. He stopped when he seemed to realize his folly, and instead cleared his throat.

"Kairnos," he said, placing an open palm against his chest. He then performed a strange gesture in which he held his left hand in front of him with a closed fist and tapped the top of it with his opposite elbow.

Taking a chance, Alex repeated the gesture and stated her name, presuming Kairnos to be his.

"Alex," she said with growing confidence in her linguistic skills.

"Allllllleeeex!" The stranger beamed, drawing out her name with a cheery tone and tilting his head upwards.

He gestured to himself once again, "Kairnos." he repeated, "Alex!" he again pointed towards her.

Alex felt like she was communicating with a caveman, a friendly one, but it was clear that despite her progress in the conversation, it might be best to bring their language expert down here now that it was confirmed to be safe.

She assumed as much at least; they had entered town about fifteen minutes ago and had not been singled out until Isaac's curiosity got the better of him.

"Alex leave," she said, making a walking motion with her index and middle finger. "Isaac? Stay." She shifted her attention to her colleague. She was still speaking slowly and simply and realized that this combined with her word choice made it sound as though she were addressing a dog.

"Sorry, wait here Isaac, I'm going to get Alicia. And please, stay out of trouble." She began a brisk walk back up the hill to the team.

The team gathered before her while Alex caught her breath.

"Everything okay down there? Looks like you were getting an earful from that big dude," said Charlie.

"That thing can see that far, that clearly?" asked Alex.

"Yes Ma'am, the miracles of modern technology."

"Yeah well, Isaac decided to do some window shopping and I had to convince a blacksmith to not cut off his fingers or whatever. There was an apparent language barrier so now that we know things seem safe I came back up here to get Alicia for translation."

Still engrossed in her tablet, Alicia's ears perked up and a smile spread across her face. "Ooh how *exciting*! My first translation, my pronunciation could use some work, but I know enough to get directions to a bathroom," she beamed.

Confused, Alex asked, "How...could you possibly know that?"

"I was part of the team that interviewed Mister John Doe, it took a while, but I got a basic gist of how their language structure worked, not all that different to English grammar actually, so he picked English up fairly well." Alicia rambled, in what Alex was realizing was her default cheery tone.

'John Doe' according to the text records, had been the only human to have come through a Rift *safely*. The UNARC took him into protective custody after he narrowly survived being shot by some very nervous, trigger-happy Swiss soldiers. After he recovered from the initial shock, both literal and cultural, they interviewed him to learn more about his language, with mild success. This was how the booklets came to be.

"Well good, you'll get a chance to use it," Alex gestured for Alicia to get going towards town.

Alicia turned to Anthony who's attention had returned to his computer equipment and snuck a kiss on his cheek before he could react. Her boyfriend seemed flustered by the display of affection.

Alex wasn't yet sure if she found their rather open affectionate interaction to be sweet or sickening. She pondered this as she and Alicia set off down the hill.

Alex had very limited experience with romance, a few crushes during middle and high school, but she never acted on them. Boys didn't really approach her, she had been taller than everyone, even back then, and her stern outward demeanor combined with her stature had made her intimidating. She had always tried not to take it personally, but it was exactly that. She hadn't really had many people outside of her family that had stuck with her long enough to see her personality beyond the calculative way she carried herself and imposing appearance.

She wasn't a particularly social person, certainly not on the level of someone like Darius, but she had met people whose company she enjoyed, in limited doses at least.

It wasn't long before Alex's internal inquisition was interrupted by the return of the sensations of the crowded town. She paid special attention to Alicia, making sure she didn't lose another teammate to the sea of strangers. Eventually they came upon Isaac, who was sitting across from the man, inspecting a sword that was rather plain in comparison to the one he had been ogling earlier.

"Sword!" Isaac said to the blacksmith.

"Ah, sword? Hur Ji'keltro tiruyan," the man responded. With the second word he gestured to the sword. It seemed like they were exchanging words for various things.

"Ji'keltro..." Isaac mused, staring at his own reflection in the shimmering blade.

"I'll take it from here Isaac." Alicia excitedly placed herself between her younger teammate and the stranger.

It was at this point that Alicia and the Blacksmith began conversing at a speed that Alex had no hope of following. The only words she understood were each of their names. After a brief conversation Alicia brought her up to speed.

"His name is Kairnos, he's the local blacksmith. He says he's happy to see foreigners like us enjoying the festival."

Alex was equal parts relieved and concerned. Relieved that she had enough intuition to figure out his name but concerned it was *that* obvious they weren't locals.

"Can you ask him if he's willing to tell us more about the town?" asked Alex.

With a short nod Alicia returned her attention to their new friend. After another bout of spirited gibberish conversation, Alicia said, "He says this is the town of Kresgroh, and they're celebrating their harvest and trade festival. Do you have any specific questions for him?"

Alex paused; it had only just occurred to her that their simple assignment to *explore* didn't include any instructions for making contact with the locals. Had she already interacted too much? Would they be in trouble if they researched further?

While Alex had this internal debate, she heard what sounded like screaming.

The nearby crowds seemed to hear it as well. They were growing increasingly uneasy, nearing panic.

A group of people came running from the edge of town, desperately shouting words that were unknown to Alex. She looked to Alicia for clarity but was met with shock on her translator's face.

It wasn't until she saw the expression on the blacksmith's face that she started to get a real understanding of what was happening. One of the words repeated most by those fleeing and screaming was "Orcs", which Kairnos shouted angrily as he grabbed a large ax from the rack nearest to his forge.

"Alicia what's going on?" Alex gestured for Isaac to get to his feet.

"The village," Alicia muttered, "is under attack."

CHAPTER 7

ALEX PUSHED AGAINST THE CROWD, forcing herself past the fleeing villagers as they ran in the direction of the rest of her team.

Her first thought was that her team might have been compromised, but she couldn't think of any rational thing that would have led them to instill such fear in the locals.

The questions in her head were swept aside when she broke through the crowd. She stared in horror at a standoff between three of the village people and five much taller, green-skinned creatures.

Some villagers were helping the injured all behind the line of defense formed by the lightly armored humans who held the creatures at bay.

Based on their shabby equipment and the sluggish way they moved, Alex surmised these were some form of volunteer guards, but regardless, the spears they jabbed at their strange enemies seemed to be holding them back, at least for now.

Isaac and Alicia came right behind Alex both seemed as shocked as she was by the sight before them.

The blacksmith Kairnos sprinted past them, nearly bowling Isaac over. She watched the burly man charge into the fight without hesitation and swing his ax at one of the green-skinned beasts. The blow landed squarely on its left side igniting a full out battle.

A monster lifted one of the guards over its head and tossed him into a market stall. Another guard jabbed the head of his spear into the chest of the biggest enemy. The spear snapped and he was slashed with the enemy's sword. Alex felt helpless but she had to decide what they should do. Would the repercussions be worse for her team if they interfered? Everything happened so fast, Alex barely had time to see Kairnos holding one of them off with his bare hands.

Kairnos had planted his ax in the first creature but was stabbed by one of them.

Alex heard a loud crack to her immediate left. She turned and reached for her holster.

Isaac's gun was drawn, and his makeshift cloak fell to the ground. In only his tactical gear, he was already off sprinting.

Isaac shouted, "KAIRNOS!"

"Isaac!" Alex knew she wouldn't get his attention. She tossed her raincoat aside, drew her weapon, and followed her younger teammate.

The monster that stabbed Kairnos was not seriously damaged, but it reeled back and dropped its weapon. Kairnos held his ground and kept the enemy at bay.

Kairnos's ax attack left an enemy on the ground; another wrestled with one of the guards over a broken spear. The last of the enemies charged the guard it had thrown into the stall.

Apparently, the loud gunshot was not a distraction and Alex hoped they wouldn't notice the advanced technology of their weapons; they were remarkably quiet for guns.

A battle was not in the plan, but Alex and her team were in the middle of it, and it did not appear negotiation was an option. Even with a bullet in it, one beast lunged towards Isaac.

Alex took aim and fired two shots. It fell backwards and crashed to the ground.

Kairnos' opponent seemed to be caught off guard by the gun

shots, and Kairnos laughed and threw a headbutt at it. The creature fumbled back and tripped over its ally who was on the ground.

Alicia had followed them, and with her own weapon drawn, she shouted something in the Rift language at the creature. It growled a terrible, gurgling sound, and lunged for her, but she used the secondary trigger on her weapon and launched two barbed prongs into its skin. Electricity coursed through the green-skin humanoid's body, and Alex was relieved to see that their tasers worked on bad guys in this world too.

Kairnos' curious expression told her it may be difficult to explain. One of the beasts was fleeing, a spearhead still in its chest. Alex fired her stun gun at the creature's back, and it fell backwards, convulsing on the ground.

The town guards quickly piled on-top of the beast to restrain it. Another creature fell with a loud thud, convulsing like the others. A moment later, Alex heard a shot echo from the top of the hill, in the direction of the rest of the team.

Charlie must be putting her *special* rifle to good use. With each of the beasts disabled or dead. Alex cautiously holstered her weapon.

Alex was relieved to find Isaac and Alicia attending to Kairnos' wounds. Their first combat had been effective, and she checked on some of the injured. The guard who was thrown into the fruit stall landed on what looked to Alex like peaches, so he had a soft landing. By this point Darius and the others arrived.

"Alex! Is everyone alright?" Darius' tone surprised Alex. It seemed contrary to his typical cheerful, almost serene demeanor. She studied him for a few seconds then said, "Apart from our friend the blacksmith I think just scrapes and bruises."

She turned to Charlie, "Did you see what happened before we got here?"

"These *things* came rushing out of the woods into the crowd! It was just brutal," she was clearly shaken.

The crowds. Alex had forgotten about the people. She searched the villagers. Many had been moved and others were being moved. She couldn't be certain from this distance, but she was convinced that a few of the people on the ground would not be getting back up.

Did they get too involved or did they not intervene early enough? The beast's sickly green skin was dry and leathery, and they were clad in pants and studded leather vests. The shortest was at least seven feet tall. All were bulky, ugly, and had large, deformed jaws filled with protruding crooked teeth.

Alex didn't turn when Kairnos said from behind her, "Orcs." She was looking at the Orc that Isaac had shot. It was motionless; almost certainly dead. A dark green liquid flowed from its wounds, presumably its blood.

"Are they always this ruthless?" Alex was talking to Kairnos, but she glared at the captured Orcs.

It took Alicia a few minutes to get back into her translator thought process, then she conveyed the message to Kairnos.

"Yes," said Alicia. "They are heartless creatures, driven only by bloodlust and hunger." Her lips quivered; she was obviously affected by all of this.

Alex had known evil. Earth had plenty of it and in her previous assignments, she had witnessed it firsthand. But ideological differences, however extreme, weren't the same as an entire species centered entirely on destruction. It was possible that Kairnos was biased, that not all Orcs were like this. Maybe these were a particularly violent faction, but deep-down, Alex had a gut feeling that wasn't the case.

Alex asked, "What do we do with them? Are there…authorities in the town we can turn them over to?"

Again, Alicia relayed Kairnos response, "The town guard will be here shortly. They'll want to take them for questioning and execution."

The word tugged at Alex like a hook in her skin. "Execution? Is there no legal system or alternative to outright execution?"

Alicia said, "No, not for Orcs, not for crimes like this."

Alex was at a loss. While it was obvious to everyone that this was an unforgivable act of violence, it was still a major realization to Alex that they were practically in the Wild West out here. Mob justice and execution was probably the best they could do to deal with what would be classified as terrorism back on Earth.

"Alex, tij ko tija hrefkr yuf Zaleevyo?" Kairnos asked Alex, or at least she thought it sounded like a question.

"He's asking if we're—something?" Alicia said, "Some sort of masters of something. The 'eevyo' in Zaleevyo usually means *'trained in'*."

Alicia asked for more details from Kairnos, and Alex checked his wound. If he wasn't such a large, burly man, the stab might have been dire, but she still felt it was too dangerous to leave him like this.

Alicia finished her conversation with Kairnos, and with a mixture of humor and confidence in her expression, she said, "He thinks we're magic."

Alex stifled a chuckle. She had not expected that reaction to their firearms.

"Kairnos," Alex said, dismissing the idea of magic. "I'd like to ask that you allow us to take you with us to our camp to get your wounds fixed up."

Alicia conveyed the message, but Kairnos looked hesitant. He glanced over at Isaac, who was now helping the volunteer guards tie up the Orc attackers. The gruff man furrowed his brow and nodded.

Alex returned the nod, cracking a genuine smile, "Good. Alright team, I think it's time we report back to home."

CHAPTER 8

After carefully backtracking to the Rift, the team emerged from the trees. It had been nearly a few days since they had left Earth. Most of their travel had been through the dense trees.

It was roughly noon, and Alex shielded her eyes against the sun high overhead. They approached the Rift, where nearly a dozen people, in the same uniform as her team, were setting up a far more sophisticated base than what they had initially brought with them.

They had used their initial tether to install what appeared to be a more capable transport system. It looked like a miniature railway with cargo containers instead of train cars.

"Senior Agent Petrakis!" Alex turned to the sound of the heavy Eastern European accent.

"Senior?"

"Yes, as of a few days ago," the man chuckled as he matched her pace walking into camp. He extended his hand, "Pyetro Zinchenko, from the Ukrainian delegation."

Alex returned the handshake and motioned to the arrivals. "Nice to meet you Pyetro, are these all your people then?"

"Oh no no, just Pyotr and Eva over there." The man cheerfully waved at a man and a woman who bore the same yellow and blue flag patch on their shoulders as he did.

Alex suppressed a chuckle. The UNARC certainly attracted talented individuals, the best in their fields, but also some unique personalities. This man wasn't the same sort of big, warm, and kind of cheerful guy that Darius was. If any word could describe Pyetro's tone it would be *'chipper'*.

"What about the rest of them?" asked Alex.

Pyetro gestured to the rest of the camp, "UK, Japan, Brazil, and of course, our Swiss hosts."

"I thought the next team would only be Norwegians?"

"When we heard about the situation on this end, less combat, more grass fields, and exploration, they sent in the logistics teams. That's us. I'm in charge of base logistics for the time being. Don't you worry, my whole country is grass fields, so I know the territory." He grinned as though he had just made a clever joke.

"What's the plan then? Is *our* mission complete?"

"Truth be told I'm not sure, I'm sure you'll get a clear answer once you've reported in. Where have you guys been by the way?"

"Our blind exploring turned out to be more time-consuming than expected. But we found a settlement, people, and unfortunately a fight." She looked back at Kairnos and his wound which still needed further attention with proper facilities.

Pyetro looked over his shoulder at the stranger, "Oh, I see you made a friend. And it looks like you already got him in some trouble." he chuckled. "We don't have a proper medical facility here yet, but we can take him through the Rift and treat him there."

Alex had been hoping to avoid that, it was one thing to take this man from his home and off into the wilderness with the promise of healing, but to then take him into another world felt more than slightly dishonest, not to mention overwhelming. Alex turned to Alicia, "Okay, this is gonna be complicated."

Alicia nodded.

Alex walked over to Kairnos. "You've been immensely helpful to us, and you are the first person I truly trust in this place. As strange as it sounds, we're not just foreigners, we came through this," she pointed to the Rift. "And we're here to learn why things are coming from your end of the Rift and attacking our world."

Kairnos looked at her curiously while Alicia translated.

Alex realized how ridiculous the entire explanation must sound, and she knew she wouldn't believe it if she were in his position.

Alicia nodded for her to continue.

"We'd like to take you *through* the Rift to our world to treat your wounds more properly. Maybe we can learn more about your language." She hoped her ever-decreasing confidence wasn't obvious to those around her as Alicia relayed the lengthy message.

Kairnos seemed more skeptical than when she asked only for him to leave the village. He was still receiving help to walk from Darius and Anthony, but, as he looked around at the strange people, his expression made it obvious he was far from comfortable with the idea.

Alex looked over to see Isaac leafing through the language booklet. He stepped in front of the blacksmith. "Kairnos...Gyu'tek!" he pleaded.

Kairnos furrowed his brow and his facial muscles tensed. His terse expression caused his beard to slightly lift. He looked at Alex, and then back at Isaac. He nodded, "Fo rhogek, tijuf req'war."

Alicia's face lit up, "He'll come!"

Alex sighed. With the weight lifted from her shoulders, she walked towards the Rift. Towards home.

Minutes later they were stepping off of a rail platform and back into their world, except Kairnos who had just left his.

A team moved Kairnos to a stretcher and took him to a medical building located in the closest part of the underground town. Alicia and Anthony went along with their blacksmith friend.

Alex and Darius reported immediately to the command building, where Darius let them in with his keycard. Alex thought she should have one of those by now.

Ahead of them, an older man sat behind a modest folding desk. He stood incredibly straight, almost a regal posture.

"Greetings, Byron, and you must be Agent Petrakis. My name is Tormod Norgaard, head of the Norwegian delegation, and subsequently this mission, as a whole."

Alex suddenly flashed back to meeting higher-ups in the Air Force. Her boss's boss, and similar arrangements. This was not something she expected to be doing right off the bat, but here she was. "Nice to meet you sir."

"Oh, stow it with the sir. Byron and I are old friends and this many countries aren't gonna get along any longer than two weeks if we're all pulling rank from dozens of different organizations." The man had only a slightly detectable accent.

Alex had met informal leaders before, but this man seemed to be more concerned with the task at hand than anything else, even if he was a bit grumpy. "Gladly Norgaard."

After listening to a detailed retelling of their time on the other side of the Rift, Norgaard sat pondering with his hands together, elbows on the desk. "So, you say these Orcs attacked random passersby? This could be a good lead to figuring out more about the attacks and the Rifts as a whole. Regardless, I do not fault you for interfering, Petrakis, I would have done the same."

"Well, actually Isaac Ross was the first to act. He defended our only contact before I had a chance to draw my weapon. He deserves any praise," Alex admitted.

"I did not give you praise, I simply said that in a very difficult situation I would have made the same decision. Ideally, you wouldn't be in that situation in the first place, but I can't fault you for being at the wrong place at the wrong time," he responded sternly.

Alex couldn't agree with that in her head, they were at the right place at the right time to help the people there, but she kept that to herself.

Norgaard continued, "It sounds like you and your team were effective in all aspects of your mission and given you are presently the most experienced group with the Rift, we're going to keep you on for further tasking. Miss Daniels is a talented linguist as well, one of our top priorities should be to establish a firm understanding of the language spoken in that region so that we can equip those journeying to the other side with automatic translation devices."

"Got it," said Alex. "What's our next assignment then?"

Norgaard ordered, "You'll establish a better understanding of a wide radius around the base camp. We need to know the terrain, even if you have to go in a grid pattern, we need it plotted out."

Everything he said made sense to Alex, but at the same time it seemed like this was too uniform of an approach to what had evidently been a very dynamic and fluid situation in the field. Not to mention it was a waste of their talents, especially Alicia's. They weren't cartographers, more importantly wouldn't a drone be able to do this much easier in a fraction of the time?

Alex opened her mouth but changed her mind. She didn't want to go against her new boss' first order, especially given how blunt she would have been.

Darius was standing close to her and gently poked her with his elbow.

Norgaard didn't notice.

Alex instinctively said, "Frankly, that seems like a waste of time and resources, especially Miss Daniels' talents. I'd ask that a drone be tasked with the mapping, and we be allowed to gain further contacts, attempt to integrate with the settlement, and get a general sense of the culture. The only consistent thing about the Rift has been its inconsistency, we haven't correctly predicted anything about the world we're dealing with here. If we're going to be able to explore effectively, I'd say sending out small teams like mine that have a smaller footprint is the best course of action." Alex was surprised at her boldness, and immediately regretted it. She was ready to receive a reprimand from the imposing man.

Norgaard cleared his throat and looked Alex directly in the eyes, "Very well, proceed with your plan in one week."

With that Darius walked forward and shook the man's hand, "It's good to see you again, Tormod. Take care of yourself."

"Byron, you dote over me more than my dear wife," Norgaard chuckled.

Darius ushered Alex out of the room quicker than she could think.

The door closed behind them. "Um. What just happened? He completely changed his mind."

"I believe you just got clearance to proceed however you want," Darius beamed.

Alex processed it all internally until it clicked. "A *test?*" she asked incredulously. "Really?"

"Oh yes, Tormod is quite fond of cutting the chaff and getting to know what people really think. Part of why he and I have gotten along so well, although I don't appreciate the sneakiness quite as much," he mused as he walked away.

Alex sighed. She was beginning to think everyone in the UNARC was some sort of eccentric.

CHAPTER 9

AFTER THEIR EXPEDITION, they spent the next week relaxing, except for Alicia. She was still trying to unravel Kairnos' language.

Alex was starting to understand her team better, at least she thought she was. She wanted to be a better leader, so she checked on them each day.

Fiercely loyal, Isaac was eager, but was adverse to sticking out, so he often seemed in conflict with himself. He was deceptively competent in his job. One thing she was certain of, he was genuine, and without an ounce of guile.

Charlie puzzled Alex the most. Every time Alex found her, she was tinkering with something. She was never with the group during lunch or dinner, nor was she in the mess hall. Talking with her was a game of chance. She said only enough to get to the end of a conversation. Unless it was something she was interested in, namely their gear or equipment; then she was like a firehose. Charlie taught Alex more about their equipment than she ever could have learned from the manufacturers.

Darius had been Alex's right-hand-man, so she knew him best, at least she hoped. On the surface he was personable and equal parts cheerful and calm; however, to get any deeper might take some work. He seemed to have a knack for reading the room and to solve conflict. Everyone seemed to like him despite his imposing figure.

Up to now, Alicia had perhaps been the most valuable member of the team. She certainly wasn't lacking in enthusiasm, and she faced their first barrier head on with her language skills.

Alex hadn't yet found much time to talk with Anthony, especially when Alicia was around. She talked more than him anyway—he seemed to be constantly checking data on his tablet. Alex did find the opportunity to speak with him one-on-one a couple of times.

Alicia and Anthony met in high school and followed each other through college, then on to the CIA. Anthony was shy, reserved, and polite. Alex knew he might end up being the least appreciated of them all. His work was seldom seen by the team, usually reserved for the higher-ups. Alex didn't have much interest in seeing atmospheric readings or soil sample reports, but still.

Alex traveled to the other side of the Rift to check on the progress of the outpost, it was coming along rapidly. By the end of the week approximately thirty people were assigned there, most stayed full time.

Pyetro had become a quick friend to Alex. Despite being in a high-ranking position in a secret expedition, he seemed proudest of the old Polaroid photos of his grandkids. He kept them with him at all times and displayed them for whoever would take the time to indulge him. His quirks aside, he was efficient, and well respected by those at the outpost. Alex thought it was most likely due to his chipper attitude, and she found something charming about his attempt to keep things light and positive.

Logistically, they were transporting tons of material through the Rift every day. Alex had overheard talk from some engineers at the mess hall that the Looking Glass facility would possibly get additional reactors to make a wider portal, although the increase would be small.

The majority of the materials had gone towards facilities to accommodate more people on the other side of the Rift. They were transporting small drones to map the surrounding area, and some light militarized ATV's for patrol vehicles. It was quickly becoming a more sophisticated operation.

On the final day of their break, Alex checked on Kairnos in the medical ward, only to find Alicia placing a mask-like apparatus on his face.

"Is he alright? What happened?"

"Oh no, it's fine, this isn't related to his injury. That actually healed quite nicely," Alicia adjusted the mask and pressed some buttons on the side of it. "Okay, try it now."

Kairnos grinned, "Hello, Alex!" His English was perfect, which shocked Alex.

An excited Alicia explained, "We're using the Universal Translator for some basic language in the Kestalian tongue so he can carry on a conversation."

"Kestalian?" Alex stared at Kairnos. His enthusiastic expression humorously obscured by the mask.

Alicia continued to fiddle with the apparatus. "Kestalian is the regional language of the Kingdom of Kestalia, through the Rift."

"Wow, you sure have made a lot of progress."

"Oh yes!" said Kairnos. "Alicia is a very smart woman, Alex. This place you have brought me to is amazing. It is great to be able to speak with you, although I don't understand how your magic works."

His voice through the mask was slightly off-putting, too cheery and he was using only basic words.

Alex had a love-hate relationship with the older handheld models of Universal Translators they used in the Air Force. It was invaluable to be able to communicate with allies naturally, but the AI-generated recreations of the voices always sounded off. This iteration of the technology sounded much better, but there was still something missing.

"We'll be getting the team some better ones soon," Alicia said.

Kairnos stood and stretched, "Alex, I would like to take you and your friends back to Kresgroh and show you around."

"We were planning to leave tomorrow but I don't think anyone is gonna fault us for heading out early," said Alex.

"Fantastic!" Kairnos practically shouted. The English language did nothing to slow down his larger-than-life personality.

CHAPTER 10

On the walk to the village Alex took the opportunity to get to know Kairnos and the area.

Kestalia was technically a kingdom, but it also had a court of nobles who had a say in how things were run. It was a relatively young kingdom, only having had four monarchs in its lifetime, but it was nonetheless a substantial country.

Kairnos admitted that he did not know much more than that himself, but he seemed to think that the capital didn't really care about small villages.

Kresgroh lay on the very edge of the kingdom's territory, and it was largely self-sufficient. Outside resources and wealth came in mostly coming from the yearly festivals.

They didn't get that kind of information from John Doe, the original traveler from the other side of the Rift. He had not cooperated much with those who questioned him; but maybe that was the problem—it had been an interrogation.

With the knowledge that their blacksmith friend had provided in such a short period of time, Isaac's theory of this being a world of medieval technology seemed more and more plausible. Kairnos told stories of fantastical creatures and claimed that magic was real in this world.

Alex learned that Karinos had been a blacksmith for thirteen of his almost thirty years. Other than occasionally traveling to study under other smiths, in neighboring villages, he had lived his entire life in Kresgroh

Alicia seemed almost disappointed that they were going back through so soon. Maybe she had hoped for more time to study the language or maybe there was a deeper issue. Alex didn't feel like she was in a position to pry about it.

When they arrived, they were greeted with a different sight than their first visit. The town wasn't nearly as crowded, and the festive decorations had been taken down. Less carts and stalls in the street, and a more laid-back atmosphere.

Kairnos explained that the two under-equipped guards on watch were volunteers. In their time off, Alex had run through their skirmish with the Orcs in her head. Alex couldn't help but respect these young men who were willing to protect their home for presumably no compensation.

She recognized one of the men. Kairnos had saved him in the first battle, and the two exchanged an enthusiastic greeting. The guards also thanked the rest of the team, at least that's what Alex thought they were saying in what she assumed was the local language. Alex simply nodded and shook the first man's hand, letting him talk as much as he wanted, and then mumbled a thanks as they all walked away.

It had occurred to her that they would fit in better with the locals if they could get some local clothes. She decided that should be their first stop.

Kairnos said the tailor's shop was in the center of town. Not a short distance, but with far less crowds it would be easier to keep track of everyone. But it was also easier to be noticed. As effective as their rudimentary disguises were in a large crowd, they stood out in the open, especially since they wore matching uniforms.

Kairnos clearly knew the shopkeeper and greeted her as a friend. Back home this place would have been an antique store.

Crude wooden mannequins sported mostly the style of clothes the villagers wore. Other racks displayed more expensive clothing she assumed were geared more toward visitors.

Alex flicked through different racks, disappointed at the lack of utility in almost all of the clothing. It would be difficult for them to walk the line between useful clothing and fitting in. Each of her team were also perusing, and Alex didn't mind having variety in their clothes, it would help them blend in.

She took a few different options to one of the dressing booths tucked in the back of the shop. Alex eventually decided on some solid pants, made of a softer leather. She chose a cotton blouse, a dark blue coat that was just the right length on one side to keep her weapon holster hidden, but still within reach.

Charlie had gone full utility, with all manner of leather straps and a solid leather vest with many pouches and pockets. Darius had similar pants to Alex, but a much larger coat. He was probably the best dressed of the group if they had been going for fancy looks. Alicia had, as Alex had predicted, gone for a gentler appearance with a loose shirt, a scarf and even a skirt in place of pants. Alex wanted to protest, but figured it wasn't worth it, and given that Alicia would usually be their first point of contact with people it was probably good that she was approachable. Anthony was similarly low-key with a button-up shirt and cloth pants with a belt. He chose a large leather satchel, presumably to stow all his science stuff. Then there was Isaac, who was *fully* enjoying their fantastical circumstance. He looked like a combination of a pirate and a knight without the armor. Once again Alex nearly protested, but he arguably fit in the best of all of them, much to her chagrin.

Still, Alex was impressed and even a bit proud at their transformation. They had entered looking like a SWAT team and were leaving fitting in, all in a bit under fifteen minutes.

When they first entered, the shop had been empty, except for the owner, but now there were half a dozen people. Some were dressed like other villagers, but some were wearing different coats, and Alex could see that under the coats there was some sort of uniform.

One woman had a dagger in a sheath. Alex wondered if they were some sort of law enforcement. To be safe, she put up her guard as she approached the counter.

Kairnos chatted with the shopkeeper who was about his age. He was casually leaning on the counter, clearly comfortable with this person. Their conversation was gibberish to Alex, except for the laughter.

Kairnos had removed his translating mask when they entered the town. It occurred to Alex that their own more advanced translators would be out of place even wearing local clothing. They were lightweight, with only a strap that connected under the ears; they didn't obstruct the face, but they did *sound* strange.

They would have to address that problem later. Right now, keeping communication open was more important.

She took her device from her bag, put it on and waited for the tone as it turned on. She had used these before, but hearing her own voice speaking a foreign language took a lot of getting used to. However, one of the features of this translator is that she could hear the conversation in English no matter what language they spoke.

She decided to test it out on the shopkeeper.

"Thanks for your help ma'am." Then to Kairnos, "I think we're all set. Did you both understand all of that?"

They both nodded.

Alex suddenly had a realization, How were they paying for this? They had no currency.

"Uh, Kairnos, we have no money from around here. Are *you* paying for this?"

Kairnos' eyes widened, and his expression changed to one of dread. "Alex, I do not have enough gold to cover all of you. I had completely forgotten that you would not have any of our currency."

He looked, sheepishly, at the tailor. "Valar, I don't suppose you would be willing to part with this merchandise as a favor for a good and appreciative friend?" He gave a halfhearted grin.

"Kairnos!" she scolded. "Outfitting strangers with fine clothing for free is not how I made this shop successful. Gold is gold, they'll need to pay *somehow.*"

Alex was about to interject when a sizable bag dropped onto the counter, making a jingling noise and a heavy thud.

"Their debt is covered." The gruff voice came from behind her, and someone grabbed her arm and roughly jerked her away from the counter.

Immediately she swept her attacker's leg, pinning him to the floor with her knee. Adrenaline and anger welled in her, but she froze when three cloaked strangers stood above her, weapons drawn. Two with daggers in-hand, and one with a crossbow pointed directly at her.

She held her attacker but looked up at them cautiously. The rest of the team were taken by surprise. From the corner of her eye, she saw Darius peeking around a clothing rack, his own weapon in hand. She subtly shook her head, attempting to warn him to hold back. The others looked more concerned than ready for a fight.

Knowing Darius had her back, Alex slowly stood.

Why would they pay for the clothes, and then immediately assault her? "What do you want?"

The man got off the floor. "Stand down, the fault is mine." He turned to Alex, "Apologies miss, clearly I'm not the best at introductions. I was hoping to get you away from any curious ears."

"That doesn't answer my question."

"Word of your actions defending this town caught our attention. I represent a wealthy merchant who is seeking safe passage to the capital. Would you consider being his guards?"

"Why would you trust complete outsiders to such a job? Aren't you capable of guarding them yourselves?"

The man looked down and sighed, "His enemies are many and powerful. We need something no one would expect. Based on what we've heard about your battle with the Orcs, it sounds like you're capable of a potent form of magic."

Alex stopped herself from laughing, "I guess the story must have gotten twisted in a game of telephone before it got to you."

The man looked confused.

"Right, telephone. Never mind. Listen, we're not magical, we're just...not from around here."

"All the more reason to have you, the way things are right now, we can't trust anyone."

Alex was intrigued, but she didn't like the vagueness of his explanations. Still, making it to the capital would give them a much greater understanding of this world.

"Give me a moment to discuss this with my colleagues," Alex returned to her team, but she didn't take her eyes off the cloaked figures.

CHAPTER 11

THE TEAM HUDDLED IN A CORNER, and Alex removed her translation set to ensure the merchant's men wouldn't understand anything she said if they were listening in.

"Boss, what's going on? Who are those guys?" Isaac whispered.

"Not sure, but they want us to escort some wealthy trader to the capital city."

Alicia's eyes lit up. "The capital? Imagine the things we could learn about the culture, the language. So much information to be obtained."

"So many ways to get stabbed in the back and left in a ditch," Charlie whispered sarcastically.

"Either way," said Alex. "I'm tempted to take the offer. We'd be getting a guide to the capital, obtaining local currency and yes Alicia is right, there is a lot to learn. What do you guys think?"

"We don't even know how far away it is. We can't just drop off the radar for a month, not without informing command," said Anthony.

"Good point," said Alex. She thought for a second. "I have an idea. I can send Kairnos to tell Pyetro. They'll know him, and he's got his translator."

Isaac twisted his mouth, "This seems kind of sketchy, but I'm not gonna say no to a real-life adventure."

Charlie rolled her eyes. "Really? You go through an interdimensional portal every other week, but a road trip is what you consider an adventure?"

Isaac shrugged sheepishly.

"So, we're in agreement then?" Alex looked at each of them.

"I say yeah," said Darius. "But we've got to be really careful about this. There are a lot of ways to attract the wrong kind of attention."

Alex nodded and put her translator back on.

"One last thing, Alex. I heard that UNARC was setting up a high-altitude balloon with a radio array in a few days," said Charlie. "Our walkie talkies should finally be useful for long distances, so we can report back to base and get instructions and we wouldn't be off the radar."

"Awesome, it's about time," said Alex.

Alex walked over to the man who had grabbed her.

"Alright. We'll escort your merchant," she said.

"Good. We leave at dawn tomorrow," and with that the man and his partners left, their pace indicating that they might need to be somewhere.

Kairnos whispered to her, "Those strangers are not from around here, Alex. They are certainly lying to you."

Alex nodded at her friend. He was right. They had to be lying about *something*, the question was *what*?

"But still, I trust you to take care of yourself and your friends. It sounds like you're not leaving till the morning, I'd like to take you all around the town!" Kairnos' grim demeanor returned to his usual cheer, and Alex's spirits were immediately lifted.

"Of course, Kairnos."

Hours later, Alex sat by an ornate fountain in the center of town. It was especially nice compared to the rest of the settlement; it was clearly a talented stonemason who had created it. The past several hours had been a whirlwind of introductions to strangers, and unfamiliar sights, smells, and concepts.

Kairnos had paraded them around the town, introducing her to each acquaintance he had in the village, no matter how minor. Everyone from the baker to the shoe cobbler

The only encounter that made a lasting impression was going to the town doctor. They visited a guard they had fought alongside a week prior who had been wounded. The man had taken a similar injury to Kairnos, but his injury was more severe making his condition worse, possibly due to the rudimentary medical knowledge of this world.

The boy seemed genuinely happy to see them. Alex felt a bit of pride for her actions, and it was all in all a pleasant interaction. The situation was made easier by her translator device, enabling them to have a conversation.

Alex wasn't sure why, but she had found introductions, however brief, to be tiring. Especially when they were back-to-back. Combined with the wealth of information she had absorbed in the past twenty-four hours, she was ready for their gallivanting around town to be over.

Still, from her position by the fountain in the center of town, she watched her friends enjoying their surroundings.

Alicia played with some children, Isaac looked like he was taking the opportunity to buy as many souvenirs as possible, all on poor Kairnos' dime. Anthony was writing *everything* down. It was obvious to Alex that Charlie, who sat alone under a tree, was even less comfortable with the non-stop socialization than she was.

Darius was nowhere to be seen. She started to wonder where he was when she felt a tap on her shoulder.

"Feeling drained?" Darius chuckled and sat next to her.

"I guess so. Kairnos doesn't slow down for anything does he?"

"No, he certainly does not. He finds out his new friends are from another world and immediately wants to tell the milkman. I like that though; he's really living his life to the fullest. I'm a bit envious if I'm being honest."

"You? Envious? That's a surprise."

"He knows what he wants out of life, he's doing it, and still enjoying the surprises. If you ask me, he's the happiest of all of us," Darius shrugged.

Alex looked at the blacksmith. Maybe it was the atmosphere of the town, joyful and carefree, or the fact that she was getting to know her team better, but Alex felt relaxed enough to speak from her heart with Darius.

"I suppose, but he reminds me so much of you, cheerful and friendly."

Darius was visibly surprised, "Thanks! I'm glad that's how you feel, I try my best." He stood and stretched. "It's important to know what you want out of life, Alex. I learned that the hard way."

Alex looked up at her friend, but he was already rejoining the others.

What did he mean by that? By any of that? Darius was a confusing person, as well as reassuring and mysterious. But one thing he said stuck in Alex's head. What *did* she want out of life?

Wasn't that obvious? Alex thought.

But she found herself without an answer. Not a meaningful one at least. Truth was she wasn't sure why she was in this situation in the first place, what had driven her to accept the secretive assignment. As much time as Alex spent in her own head, she didn't dive very deep into her own emotions unless prompted. Even just *thinking* that made her uncomfortable.

She shook the thoughts away and focused instead on the simple pleasure of watching the sunset shine through the trees, and the dazzling colors of the shimmering fountain water.

CHAPTER 12

A CLOAKED FIGURE APPROACHED Alex not long after the sun went down. "It is time. Gather your people," the mysterious woman spoke in a hushed voice.

The woman glared at Alex from beneath the hood of the cloak. She stood to retrieve her companions.

Isaac took some convincing, but after a while he went with the rest of the team who had bid their goodbyes to Kairnos and followed the cloaked bodyguard towards the edge of town.

Alex asked, "Where are the rest of your people?"

The woman kept walking.

Alex understood the situation. Giving out information was below the stranger's pay grade, or at least that was the impression Alex got. She had dealt with the 'strong and silent security' type of people in the military, although this felt a bit more frustrating.

The rest of the team mused about their experiences as they walked, but when they approached a field on the edge of town, the conversation died.

Tents, and a large, ornate pair of wagons, surrounded a huge bonfire. The bright fire illuminated the entire camp and appeared to be the only light for miles. Alex was greeted by the man who had given her the offer. She presumed he was the leader.

"Your people may rest wherever; we only ask that you be ready to fight. Sleep well, the journey is long," the man, still fully cloaked, walked toward one of the wagons.

Alex had concluded that the guards must have a good reason to constantly wear those heavy cloaks, secrecy was obviously a concern. Two of them slept in small tents, still fully dressed in their face-covering cloaks and sheathed swords.

Her team set up their camp about fifty feet away from the others. She still didn't trust these people any more than before, so she had the team huddle together to set up a schedule to keep watch.

Alex took the second shift. She set up her sleeping bag, crawled inside, and tried to fall asleep. She had always found it hard to sleep without music, so while back home she had downloaded some of her favorite songs to her wrist computer. It played through her translation device, vibrations only she could sense. She could listen to both the comforting music and her surroundings at the same time. She knew she had to sleep with one ear open.

Alex woke to a poke from Isaac's boot and begrudgingly got up to take her watch. Alex had never seen a night sky this clear back on earth; the stars formed a canopy all around her. One glaring detail was obvious to her—the constellations *were* different, just as Anthony had said when they first came through the rift.

She watched them slowly crawl across the sky, focusing on one formation in particular; it helped her keep track of time. As she neared the end of her watch, Alex saw movement in the distance. Her eyes narrowed, trying to make out movement in the darkness. She could see a dark figure sneaking away from the other camp. She made her way over to Darius' tent and shook him awake.

"I thought Charlie had the next watch?" he grumbled groggily.

"She does, but one of the guards is sneaking out of their camp," Alex whispered urgently, still trying to keep her eye on the figure.

Darius stood, "Okay, I'll take watch, you go investigate?"

Alex nodded and hurried away.

Soon she was sneaking into town, chasing after a hooded silhouette who was wearing a cloak that was different enough it made it easy to see. The person suddenly stopped at the fountain in the center of town and simply sat down.

What was going on?

It may have been late in the evening, but the town was still very much awake. People walked about, trading and bartering, still active enough to allow her to blend in. Alex debated whether or not to stalk the stranger, watching for their next move, but with Darius on guard at camp she felt a sense of urgency to not leave her team hanging.

She walked forcefully towards the figure, but it jogged away towards the woods.

Alex pursued, but as soon as they left the crowd the stranger broke into a full run. Alex knew she had been spotted, but followed suit, her long legs carrying her decidedly faster than her target. They had just entered the woods when she overtook the cloaked figure and brought them to the ground.

She flipped the person over and Alex pulled the hood off coming face to face with a young man.

"Please! I can give you a great deal of gold if you only let me go free!" he pleaded.

That's a really weird thing for a trained and grizzled bodyguard to say.

She pressed him for answers, "Who are you?"

"That is not important! Well it is, but I cannot tell you!"

The sheer panic in his voice caused Alex to let up on the man. He stood and *thoroughly* dusted himself off. He wasn't as young as she thought he was, based on his stature he was close to her age. But with a young and soft face that didn't look like he had ever seen a fight or perhaps even a frown.

The first question she asked would result in an obvious answer;

this had to be the well-off merchant that she had been hired to protect.

The merchant finished wiping off his clothing.

"Right," he said, looking satisfied that his cloak was free of soil. "Well, farewell then," and he started to walk away.

"Hey!" Alex growled and she tackled him again.

"Will you *stop* doing that?" The man yelled, finding himself once again face-first in the dirt.

"You can't just walk away!" she hissed. "Why were you sneaking out of camp?"

"You have been following me all the way from camp? Oh, quite stealthy aren't you?" the man said as he turned over onto his back, unamused with the repetitive nature of his situation.

Annoyed, Alex had expected a lot of scenarios from this encounter but none of them included this much sass.

"Can you just answer *one* of my questions, oh Mister merchantman?" She struggled to keep her voice down.

"Oh, um, yes. I am a merchant you see. Very wealthy and successful. I left the camp because I needed to…find my shoe?"

"Right," Alex was unamused. "Let's go ask your guards then."

She helped him off the ground.

"No! Please wait! I can't ever get away from them, this is my only chance to just live a *normal life."*

Alex almost scoffed but restrained herself. By the sounds of it this guy had a way better life than *normal.* He could live any life he wanted; with his wealth he could hire a team of bodyguards. Still, the man was clearly distressed by the situation, and Alex did feel a bit of pity for having tackled him—twice.

"Fine," she relented. "We'll stay out here, but *only if* you answer my questions."

The man furrowed his brow, "Those that I can, I shall Madame."

"Deal, and don't call me Madame," Alex snapped. The man nodded and took a seat on the ground. "Ask away Mad-...Miss."

Alex sighed and sat down. At least she'd be getting *some* information this way, and he did seem a lot easier to get anything out of than his guards.

"So, assuming that my previous questions are off the table," Alex grumbled as she thought of other questions. "Who is after you?"

The man was quiet and put a hand to his chin, as if to figure out what to say. "Well, many people, but generally assassins hired by my worst enemies." He seemed rather pleased with his answer.

Alex sighed and shook her head. "That's not very helpful, generally when someone is worried about being assassinated they would be worried about assassins."

The merchant had a look of realization, as though Alex had just spoken great wisdom. Alex was starting to feel like she had been too hasty, maybe they weren't being dishonest, just discreet. Maybe she shouldn't have left Darius on guard just so she could have this stupid conversation with this dumb merchant.

She closed her eyes realizing she would likely get nothing useful out of this guy.

They listened to crickets as silence hung around them awkwardly for several moments,

"What about you?"

"What *about* me?" Alex didn't care that she was no longer whispering.

"Well, who are you? Where are *you* from?" he demanded.

Really? She opened her eyes and glared at him. "I'm one of the extra guards your men hired."

"Oh splendid, I can tell you are quite good at your job if I may say," he said matter-of-factly. He now acted as though he hadn't been tackled twice in the past few minutes.

"Thanks," Alex said, deciding it wasn't worth being mad over someone this clueless. "I guess."

"Well, where are you from then?"

"Um..." Alex realized she couldn't answer his question, at least not in detail.

"I'm from Missouri." Technically she was not lying.

"Fascinating! Miz-oo-ree, an exotic and foreign land if ever I have heard of one."

Alex chuckled. She felt bad for messing with him, but she figured that given the trouble he had put her through she had earned it.

"So, you have traveled quite some way. Across the ocean even?"

"Oh, further than that."

"Amazing. Multiple oceans. I have learned much of the world, but my scholars tell me there is so much yet that even they do not know."

Alex relaxed and closed her eyes, fighting to keep from dozing off.

"Yep, well they don't know anything about where I'm from."

"A hidden land then? Far from prying eyes. Oh, this is so exciting, tell me what your people's purpose is here?"

The UNARC had two goals: Explore and find a way to stop the Rift attacks. She figured he only needed to know the first one.

"Exploration. We seek to know more about your land."

"And what of you? What is *your* purpose?"

Alex's eyes opened once again, her thoughts returning to Darius asking the same question earlier, well a similar one at least.

"My purpose?" she pondered aloud, not to the merchant so much as to herself. Something changed in Alex's mind. A vault of emotions, cracking ever so slightly open, led her to think about things she hadn't thought of in years.

"I...wish I knew," she said.

The merchant's expression shifted to genuine confusion. "What do you mean? How could you not know?"

Alex looked at him. He seemed kind, and a bit clueless, but genuine. They had led *very* different lives, but he was still a person, so maybe he could relate. She had nothing to lose by speaking her mind, if she embarrassed herself she'd simply deliver him to the capital without saying another word.

"I thought I did once," Alex admitted, her mind going back in time as she told her tale to the stranger sitting across from her.

CHAPTER 13

"I WAS IN A MILITARY FORCE," Alex began, straining to figure out how to explain it without raising too many questions. "I was in charge of a special transport that moved people in and out of battle."

The merchant's eyes widened but he didn't interrupt.

"When things got really bad in other countries, we took our transports in to rescue people. Two countries were at war, and my job was to rescue a group of villagers from the top of a tall building." Alex's words were automatic at this point. Emotionally, she couldn't stop until she had said everything she needed to say.

"While hovering, we were lifting people onto the transport but..." she choked. "The building was attacked and collapsed. People grabbed onto the person who was being brought up, but the weight was too much and all of them fell. My friend who was bringing them aboard went down with them."

Alex stared solemnly at the ground, and they both sat in silence for several minutes.

"Miss, I'm...truly sorry. I cannot imagine..."

He seemed genuinely concerned, but also confused.

"If I may ask, why are you telling *me* this? We are strangers."

Alex shrugged; who knows? She hadn't even told her parents.

"I guess there's less risk this way. You and I will likely never speak again, we'll get to the capital and part ways." Alex looked at the ground. Why was she able to share this with a complete stranger and not the people closest to her? She berated herself internally.

What's wrong with me?

"I understand. Sometimes the people we feel we can trust are the ones we know the least," he agreed.

More silence.

"Miss, I didn't catch your name."

She looked up, "Alex. Just call me Alex."

"Miss Alex, your candor inspires me."

Alex heard a snap and looked in that direction; some leaves were stirring.

"I believe you are honest and good of heart, despite the fact that you repeatedly subdued me. I believe…"

Alex leapt to her feet and shoved him aside—she felt a rush of air when something whizzed past her, then a loud thud hit a tree behind them. She drew her weapon and fired a blind taser shot in the direction of the rustling leaves. Instantly, sparks from the taser prongs illuminated the area sporadically, like a strobe light. Alex missed the attacker with her first shot, but now with the light she could see them. She was looking right at the woman with the crossbow from their encounter at the tailor's shop, the one who had led them here.

She had almost loaded another bolt when Alex tackled her, scrambling in the dark as the woman fought back in a frenzy, kicking and attempting to headbutt her.

Normally, Alex would have won due to sheer size difference, but this woman had no lack of tenacity. Eventually, Alex was able to grapple the guard and slam her against a tree, knocking her out. Exhausted and covered in mud, Alex's arms hurt, and she felt more pain on her legs. Turning her attention back to the merchant, she found him practically cowering on the ground.

He yelled, "My word! What is happening?"

"One of your guards just tried to assassinate you. Thought that was fairly obvious," Alex rolled her eyes.

Now it was clear to Alex that his enemies were dangerous. They were actually recruiting his own guards. Maybe the guard leader was right in seeking their help.

"That's not possible, the guards love me. I assure you this is all a misunderstanding. I-I..." He was losing his composure, his goofy naivety suddenly shattered before her eyes.

Does he really believe that?

"My Liege!" That familiar gruff voice called out.

"Liege?" asked Alex.

The man ran up to the merchant. "Sire, are you harmed? Henfra was not to be trusted, and I knew it. I just didn't have the resolve to act on it for chance I was wrong," The lead guard admitted.

"Hold on," Alex interjected "Sire?"

"Calt'fors, what is *she* doing here?" One of the words he spoke did not translate, but she was quite sure he was cursing.

"Calm, Fraygor, she can be trusted." The merchant got to his feet. "Do you understand?"

The guard grumbled, but kneeled and uttered a formal, "Yes, Prince Calseous."

She finally knew exactly *how* they were lying.

Darius burst through the brush, weapon drawn. "Alex, what's going on?"

Alex immediately moved next to him.

She glared at the merchant. "Why don't you ask our friend the *prince*? They've been lying to us this whole time."

Darius' anger flared but was immediately overpowered by his naturally calm demeanor. He still confronted them.

"Explain!" he demanded of the prince and his guard.

The one called Fraygor explained as he observed the unconscious body of the would-be assassin. "His Liege Prince Calseous has many enemies in the court, and it seems not even the ranks of the royal guard can be trusted."

The prince was distraught. "That can't be, people in the court disagree with me, but the other guards could not have been made to kill me on their behalf! This is a hex, a curse of some sort, it's the only explanation."

Alex was surprised that the prince was practically pleading with his bodyguard.

She frowned, "Regardless of the cause, you guys lied to us and evidently you can't even trust each other. I think our business is concluded. Come on, Darius."

She stormed away with Darius in tow.

I'm so stupid. I can't believe I opened up to that buffoon.

"What happened?" Darius asked.

Alex grumbled, "I chased him, he got cagey when I asked him questions. One of his guards tried to kill us. That's all."

"Okay, I would have believed you if you hadn't said 'that's all'. Now what's up?"

Alex ignored him and just kept walking.

"Alex!" Darius grabbed her shoulder and turned her around, stopping her in her tracks. "What's wrong? Seriously."

Alex gritted her teeth, but she wasn't mad at Darius.

"It's just—I told him about myself. Something I shouldn't have trusted anyone with."

"Are we compromised?"

"No, they don't know about Earth or anything like that. I feel like *I've* been compromised though," she said before she started walking again. She could tell Darius wanted to say more, but he followed her and kept quiet the rest of the way back to camp.

Alex walked into their makeshift camp and shouted at her groggy teammates. "Pack up your stuff. We gotta find a place in town to stay!" She stormed into her own tent and started packing. She heard Darius explaining the situation to the others.

"Uh, boss?"

Alex spun around, “Yes? What’s up, Isaac?”

“Why are we giving up on the quest?”

Alex shot back, “Well, Isaac, they lied to us, and we can’t trust them if they’re stabbing each other in the back. And don’t say *quest.*”

“Alex, shouldn’t we be staying involved if this guy really is the prince of this country? It’s a great opportunity for information.” This time it was Charlie.

Alex turned to see her entire team.

“I thought I told you guys to pack up.”

Lacking her typical enthusiasm, Alicia said, “She’s right guys, let’s just go home.”

“Alicia?” Anthony looked at her.

Isaac glanced at Anthony, but looked quickly back to Alex. “Boss, what happened with the prince?”

Alex scanned all of their faces. “It sounds like Darius told you already.”

No one said anything.

She shrugged. “We just can’t trust him, that’s all. It was a mistake to do that in the first place.”

“But we can trust each other, can’t we?” said Isaac. “That should be enough.”

Alex wanted to snap at him, but it didn’t come out that way. “Do you really trust me, Isaac?”

Without hesitation Isaac nodded, “I do, I trust all of you.”

Alex barely knew these people. Could she really trust them?

Uncertain tension hung in the air, and for nearly a full minute no one said a word.

Anthony cleared his throat, “I never met my mom. She brought me home from the hospital to my dad in the middle of the night, and left without saying a word,” he looked at the ground.

Alicia put her hand on his shoulder.

Alicia sighed. "I'm having a hard time being here, there is a lot more violence than I expected. It's more intense than I thought it would be."

Alex was beginning to understand where this was going.

Isaac grinned, "I got rejected from the army twice before they let me in. I had to fight harder than most. But now I'm here!"

All eyes looked expectantly at Charlie.

"Don't look at me like that, I'm not spilling my guts over the campfire like some sorta hippy!" She crossed her arms, stared each of them down for a few moments, then a heavy sigh escaped her chest.

"Fine. I got bullied so much in school that I faked being chronically sick so I could be homeschooled. My parents didn't care enough to actually teach me anything, so I had to teach myself." She rolled her eyes. "Happy?"

Isaac smiled and turned to Alex,"And you, boss?"

While Alex had been moved by this moment of mutual reverent honesty, she was still hesitant to share anything with anyone after her folly with Prince Calseous.

She looked up, her eyes shifting between her team members. "I…lost people in the Pacific War a few years ago. Just before the end, when the enemy got desperate. I couldn't have done anything, I don't blame myself, it just feels unfair," Alex choked, the impact of telling them felt even more real than sharing it with the prince.

Maybe Isaac was right, maybe she *could* trust them that way. They had forged their bonds in conflict and uncertainty just like she had. "It's hard to open up again," she said. "I'm afraid that if I invest my emotions in anyone, if I lose them, I'll just get hurt again."

Now Darius placed his hand on her shoulder, "When I was deployed, I hadn't seen my family for a long time. On the flight home, all I thought about was seeing them. But I got off the plane to a dozen messages," he tried to hold back tears. "My wife and daughter had been in a car accident. My wife died in the crash, and I sat by my daughter's hospital bed for days, she never got out of it. She never woke up."

That awkward silence returned.

Isaac looked at the ground and Alicia and Anthony found comfort in each other. Charlie looked like she felt bad for her snarkiness earlier, and Alex didn't know what to say, if anything.

Darius broke the silence. "We all have a past, Alex. Something we've been through or are going through. Things we've lost. That doesn't mean we can't keep growing, finding new things, even though we risk losing them. But some of those things might be worth that risk. I told you I try my best to be friendly to everyone, to lift their spirits. I do that for my little girl, I do that because she saw the best in me. I can't let her down; I can't be any other way. That's how you honor the lost things, Alex, by moving forward."

Darius patted her shoulder and stepped back towards the others.

"For what it's worth, boss, I think all of you are worth the risk," said Isaac. "And…I'll try my best to be worth it too."

Alex had never appreciated her team more than she did at this moment. She gave them a weary smile and nodded.

The team immediately returned to breaking down the camp, then they sought out Kairnos in town. He offered his home for them to rest in their sleeping bags.

Changing locations in the middle of the night left them little time for sleep. At first light they said goodbye to Kairnos and made the trip back to the Rift.

Alex's emotions were raw, and she felt the tension among her team.

Pyetro's smiling face as he waved her down was a welcome reprieve as they approached the outpost.

“Alex! Your blacksmith friend said you would be gone for some time. Is everything alright?”

“Yes, we’re fine, just got a bit swindled is all. I’ll tell you more about it later,” she was relieved to be in happy company.

Darius usually presented that cheerful presence that lifted others, but had been absent in their trip back, so seeing Pyetro made her smile. It seemed like the whole outpost was especially lively, with people walking around at a brisker pace than usual.

“Is something going on?” Alex asked Pyetro.

“We just got a *massive* shipment, with more on the way. All sorts of equipment, some new buildings; we’re still sorting through it. I have a feeling you will particularly enj–”

Someone shouted Pyetro’s name, followed by frantic shouting in the Ukrainian language. Suddenly, the whole camp was in commotion, all centered on the Rift. Pyetro ran towards the voice and Alex followed.

Her Ukrainian was rusty; she couldn’t have heard them right, but as she turned a corner, she knew she had.

Alex hadn’t even considered this nightmare—The Rift was *closing*.

One of the rail transports was slowly trudging through the narrowing opening, its passengers rushing through the Rift and trying to dive off. Suddenly their only way home snapped shut, cutting a cargo container in half.

A sudden silence fell across the entire base. They were stranded.

CHAPTER 14

Shock coursed through Alex's body. A million questions popped into her head, but no answers.

What now?

The question gnawed at her and left a pit in her stomach.

Pyetro cursed under his breath in his native tongue.

"What just happened?" asked Alex.

Pyetro headed toward those who had narrowly escaped.

Alex needed answers, and immediately turned to her science experts, "Alicia, Anthony, what is happening?"

Alicia's face was white as a ghost, and Anthony looked just as confused as Alex felt.

For the first time since Alex had met Anthony, he seemed truly stumped.

Alicia ran forward, "NO!" she screamed as if pleading to the Rift itself.

That seemed to shock everyone into motion and panic broke out across the base camp. Some rushed to the aid of the injured and some had fallen to their knees in defeat.

She hadn't the faintest clue how the Rifts worked, and she was certain that no one else did either.

They were really stuck here.

Darius said from behind her, "Alex, we need a plan." She had never seen Darius so serious.

"I agree, but *what* that is isn't exactly clear to me right now."

Charlie joined them, "It's a shot in the dark, but I'd say we go find that prince. He's the most important person we've come in contact with, he must know someone who can help, or at least be able to point us in the right direction."

She was right, but as pragmatic as Charlie's suggestion was, Alex was not looking forward to seeing Prince Calseous again, much less relying on him. Still, their only other option was to ask Kairnos, who, other than stories he had heard, already said he knew nothing about the Rifts.

"Pyetro!" Alex called. She found him helping a woman up off the ground. It appeared she had a concussion. "We need transport. Are the patrol buggies still around?"

"I have people here I need to take care of, but you take anything you need. If anyone is gonna solve it, it's you guys." Pyetro said.

Alex nodded and started to walk away.

"Alex," Pyetro grabbed her shoulder, and she turned around.

"I have a family, Alex. A wife, children, and grandchildren. I need to return to them. Get us home, I can trust you with this, yes?"

Joy had left Pyetro's face and the change in his demeanor startled Alex.

"I promise, Pyetro," she tried to reassure him.

An hour later, they were gathered up around a pile of gear. The entire base had volunteered their equipment and food to set them up for their journey to locate the prince. They offered their only forms of transport—two all-terrain vehicles that had been used to patrol the perimeter. They were open-air with no armor. Completely gutted, they were just a chassis and a roll-cage. One was equipped with a small, but powerful twenty-millimeter cannon on a remote-control turret.

They had one long-range radio. Alex was told it should enable them to communicate with Pyetro and the base.

Alex was relieved the vehicles were electric and had with them the charging equipment—a massive solar sheet and a set of panels that folded up into a compact stack and opened into a large flexible sheet of solar energy.

Alex solemnly looked across their equipment and the supply of food. The precedence of the sacrifice that her colleagues had made weighed heavily on her. So much of what little they had in this entire world was given to her team in hopes that they would reconnect them to their home, and it was a lot to take in.

"Pyetro," Alex turned to her friend. "I'd recommend you send your own people into the village to find a food source, just in case we don't find a solution to our situation before you run out."

Pyetro nodded but didn't make eye contact. He stared at the empty space where the Rift had been. The feeling in the air was solemn, especially amongst those who had been setting up. She and her team spearheaded the operation but spent a lot of time off in the unknown.

Those at the camp frequently made daily trips back to Earth. The communication lines had been set up just hours prior to the Rift closing, and the camp briefly even had internet.

Alex imagined people sending messages to their loved ones, the people they had left behind for this secret assignment.

Alex heard Alicia yelling.

"No, no Anthony this is not some simple problem to solve!" Alicia sobbed and buried her face in her hands. "We are *trapped* here, and we don't know if we'll ever go back home!"

Anthony had his hands on Alicia's shoulders. "I don't know what else to say dear....I just feel like it's going to work out. I'm sorry."

Alicia was seated on a pile of stacked pallets and Alex walked over to them and knelt down to be on her same level.

"Alicia, are you alright?"

Alicia's expressions were a mixture of anguish, confusion, and sorrow.

"Alex, I signed up to study a language no one had ever seen before, not fight monsters and be trapped in another world. This isn't what I'm meant to be doing."

Then it hit Alex. When she learned the pair was CIA, she had assumed they were experienced in the field, but that was a biased assumption to make.

"You're not used to this, are you? The whole fighting bad guys and heading off into the unknown thing."

Alicia threw her hands in the air. "No! I am supposed to be bringing our understanding of a new culture forward. Nobody said anything about all of…*this!*"

We are trapped here. Not just stuck, or delayed, but trapped, the wording couldn't be any more accurate.

Alex let that set in, would she ever see her family again? Would she have to live the rest of her life in this world? The scale of the problem became apparent for the first time.

Alicia was still sobbing. Alex opened her mouth to say something but stopped. She was going to agree with Alicia, but decided that's not what she needed right now.

"Alicia,…listen I know this isn't what you expected; frankly, neither did I. I didn't know anything about the Rifts at all before I got to the Looking Glass. But if there is one thing that I've learned from working with you since we got here, is that you are *invaluable*. You are our greatest asset because we need you to explain this world to us. I know you want to go home badly, and it'd be easy to shut down, but we can't do it without you. We need you for this."

Alicia's sobbing turned to sniffles. Alex wasn't sure whether it was her words or the implication behind them, but it was clearly having some effect.

Alicia looked down and wiped away some tears with her sleeve, "Alright. I…I understand. Just, give me some time."

Alex nodded and rested a hand on her teammate's shoulder before standing and heading over to the buggies.

CHAPTER 15

Charlie was precariously squatting on top of the armed buggy, fiddling with the cannon system.

"That was a good job, Alex. She's really hurting," Darius gave her an approving nod before walking away. Just like Pyetro, Alex noted a lack of enthusiasm behind Darius' words.

The entire camp was mired in a sullen, uncertain mood, and it left Alex unsettled. More motivation for her to bring them all home. She had to get that cheer back.

Within the hour, they were mounted up. Darius and Alex were in the lead vehicle with Isaac and the others following behind in the armed buggy.

"Where to?" Darius asked.

"The village. We need to tell Kairnos the situation. Maybe he can help the people at the outpost while we're gone."

The trip was much faster on wheels than it had been on foot, even with the added distance around the forest. The plan to map the local area with drones had gone well and they were easily able to navigate to the village, although their mapped area didn't extend far beyond that.

The buggies stopped atop the hill where they had first discovered the village. Despite the severity of the situation, Alex still felt it was best to keep their origins a secret, and riding into town on *'metal carriages'* or whatever the locals would call them, they certainly would be asking questions. They didn't have time for that. With Alicia's help, Alex explained the situation to Kairnos.

"This is troubling news my friends; I wish that I could be more helpful," said Kairnos.

"Maybe you can," Alex said through her translator. "We need you to take care of our people at the outpost. Help them get food, stay safe, that sort of thing."

Kairnos beamed, "Yes! Of course, Alex. As Isaac taught me, a friend of mine is a friend of yours!"

"Close enough," Alex smirked "Thanks Kairnos, I'm glad I have someone I can trust with this."

Alicia seemed at least *slightly* better when they bid the blacksmith goodbye. Alex hoped she understood that they really did need her.

The team set off in the general direction of the capital, following a rough road that Alex assumed had been blazed by carts and on foot. Traveling along the countryside of this untainted land was relaxing and a welcome change of pace.

Darius drove, with Isaac in the rear seat. The sky was filled with fluffy white clouds and didn't seem to threaten poor weather. It seemed like springtime, just like Earth.

They passed fields of crops, with farm houses nestled beside them. The air was thick with the scent of tilled ground and plant life, along with some less pleasant smells that came from the occasional livestock they passed. The creatures she assumed were cows looked a bit strange, but she couldn't see them very well.

Something in the road caught her eye. "Darius, do you see that?"

"I see it, what should we do?"

Alex gripped her radio, "Charlie, what do you see up ahead?" She knew looking through the camera on the cannon, Charlie could see clearer and farther than she could.

Charlie's voice crackled through the radio, *"Looks like a fight, boss."*

Alex cautioned her colleague, "Isaac, sidearm."

A moment later he was ready, weapon in hand.

Alex followed suit, and as they approached, she got a better understanding of the situation. Ahead of them was the remainder of the prince's guards, engaged in fierce fighting with similarly cloaked figures.

Fraygor, the leader of the guards, stood in front of Prince Calseous, his sword clashing repeatedly with one of the attacker's. Darius swung the vehicle around allowing Alex and Isaac to dismount, both firing their stun guns at the prince's aggressors.

Two of the four enemies were detained with tasers, and the fight suddenly halted, save for the clicking noise the electrodes produced. The other two were convulsing from the effect of weapons and looked at the wielders in shock and fear.

"Magic! Flee!" one shouted as she ran. Another attempted to do the same but was stopped in his tracks by a swift kick to the core from Fraygor's heavy boot.

The prince lay in shock on the ground behind Fraygor, who seemed to be the only guard left standing. The other two lay motionless on the ground.

"Darius! Get Anthony over here with medical," Alex shouted.

Before Darius could radio it in, the other buggy slowed to a stop beside him.

Alex left her team and approached Fraygor with her weapon lowered.

"I thought you had all abandoned us," said Fraygor, his stern expression unphased.

Alex wasn't in the mood for attitude, "Just be grateful our situation has changed. What happened?"

"Exactly what I feared—assassins. Many more than we were prepared for under normal circumstances, much less one guard short," he grumbled.

"Miss Alex!" The prince jumped to his feet. "I knew you and

your friends would come. Your magic is truly a wonder to behold, Mizooree must be a remarkable land."

Alex grimaced. The last time she had spoken to the prince had been a difficult conversation. But he acted as though nothing had happened then. He might not have known about the Rift closing, but she thought he would have at least taken his own attempted assassination seriously.

"It's not magic…" Alex started, but she realized there were more important things to discuss. "We need your help. What do you know about the Rifts?"

Calseous and Fraygor seemed to be confused by that word. Luckily, Alicia approached.

"Greetings, Prince Calseous! I am Alicia, a humble translator." She repeated the strange salute Kairnos had given them on their first meeting. The prince returned a similar, albeit notably different salute, while Fraygor simply copied Alicia.

"Please, we need your help, we have come through a strange gap in the air, but this passage has closed, and left us and our compatriots marooned in your land," Alicia was speaking rather theatrically, but it seemed to be working on the prince, whose eyes were wide and enthralled by her tale.

Fraygor on the other hand raised an inquisitive eyebrow.

"What do you know about these gaps as Alicia calls them?" asked Alex.

"Fraygor?" Calseous looked at his guard.

"Nothing, my liege, truthfully this is the first I've heard of such a thing."

Alex furrowed her brow, she had no reason to trust anything any of these people said, but at the same time they were her only path towards learning more. "We need to learn more about them, so we can go home."

Calseous eyebrows shot up, "You mean to tell me Mizooree is another world entirely?"

"No! It's just a state, ugh, it doesn't matter!" Alex was frustrated with this buffoon, asking silly little questions despite their dire situations. *How naive is he?*

"We need to know as much as we can, is there some sort of expert in the capital?" asked Darius.

Fraygor narrowed his eyes, "Royal scholars, perhaps, but I can promise nothing. What's more, we owe you nothing of the sort until you've fulfilled your mission to protect his majesty."

Darius and Alex shared a glance, then Alex glared at Fraygor.

"Fine. We will accompany you to the capital and you will help us get home. Seem fair?" she extended her hand.

Fraygor looked at her hand, then directly into her eyes. "Agreed," he turned to the prince and appeared to be checking for injuries.

Alex retracted her offered hand, wondering if she'd ever learn how to properly communicate in this world. If they really were trapped here forever, she'd have to learn—sooner or later.

Alex looked around and noticed Anthony giving the two royal guards medifoam. Alex hated the stuff. It was an amazing medical breakthrough for sure. It could save the person from even dire gunshots. The drawback, however, was that it was sometimes more painful than the injury.

Both guards cried out in pain. The sizzling foam reminded Alex of the stinging pain it conveyed.

Fraygor looked skeptical, "Your healing magic seems to be hurting my subordinates." He approached the guard that Anthony was attending to.

"It's painful, yeah, but it'll save them a lot of trouble in the long run," Anthony focused on the treatment.

Alex wasn't sure what to make of Fraygor. Clearly, he was capable, and he carried an aura of responsibility about him. At the same time, he didn't seem to trust them very much and Alex had little reason to trust him back, especially given the fact that another of the prince's guards had already been at her throat.

"Miss Alex?" the prince interrupted her musing.

"What is it?"

"You will accompany us to the capital, yes? This is wonderful news. There is much to see, it is a noble city of rich history, I assure you." The prince wore an odd expression. His usual naive optimism was tainted by…some emotion?

Stealing a glance back at the others, she realized she was alone with the prince.

"Listen here your majesty," Alex said. "What I told you doesn't leave your lips, otherwise you'll have worse problems than a couple of cutthroats with swords."

The prince's eyes widened, and he nodded, but he looked dejected.

Alex walked back to the buggy. She hadn't meant to be rude, just intimidating. She admitted to herself that she was not in a good mood, although it seemed none of them were. She still lamented her decision to confide in the prince, but she certainly couldn't have predicted that they would be needing him so desperately.

Alex recognized the sound of heavy boots and turned to see Fraygor running a hand across the metal surface of their transports.

"Remarkable. I must admit I'm curious how this works, but I imagine it's more complicated than even you understand," Fraygor said to Alex.

Alex squinted, wondering if that was an insult.

"I recognize a soldier when I see one in action, Miss. You do not carry yourself as a mage would." He didn't take his eyes off of the vehicle.

"What's a mage?"

"A magic user, a scholarly type. Not something I recognize in you; you are decisive, tenacious," Fraygor said, before continuing.

"I must warn you—you are entering a delicate game of deception and dueling loyalties. That much should be obvious, but I will make one thing clear to you. If your loyalties do not remain steadfastly with Calseous, you will not receive your aid."

Alex should have felt offended, but the calmness of the man's speech was somewhat reassuring, at least she was being kept in the loop now, to a degree. It was a start.

"My loyalties lie with my people, but your help is the only way I can get them home. I promise you I won't stop till I solve this," she said flatly.

Fraygor cracked a smile, betrayed by the stern position of his brow. "Perhaps, we are not so foreign to one another, at least not in character," he walked away the heavy footfalls of his boots trudging through the dirt.

Maybe this won't be so bad.

CHAPTER 16

THE SKY WAS DIM, *stormy, lit only by the shimmer of Rifts, dozens of them. From them poured throngs of terrifying creatures, all spreading to cause chaos. Her teammates were in trouble. Anthony was trapped under debris and Alicia was helping him. Darius was fighting off throngs of faceless monsters, while Isaac and Charlie desperately tried to pry open a door for them to escape.*

Immobilized and helpless, Alex watched her friend's struggle. A collapsing building rained down concrete on her.

Alex sat up gasping for air, cold sweat dripping from her brow. She didn't usually dream let alone nightmares, but everything was starting to get to her.

They had opted to set up camp not far from the ambush site, primarily to give the wounded time to rest. Charlie set up the turret of their buggy on something she called a *sentry* mode.

Alex looked outside. The faintest shimmer of stars still bleeding through the atmosphere, and slowly being wicked away by the increasing sunlight. Her wrist computer said it was around 6 AM, but she wasn't sure how accurate they were. Charlie said they were getting time the same way as sundials did way back when.

Not exactly encouraging.

Alex peeked out of her tent, relieved to see no signs of commotion. In fact, it seemed everyone was still asleep.

A pair of regal boots were hanging from the prince's fancy wagon. She approached him as he sat on a sort of bench near the front, half-tucked inside the lush interior.

"Hello, Miss Alex."

"What's wrong?" Alex noted a lack of his usual enthusiasm.

"I'm fine; do not worry," he said.

He's lying.

Alex hoisted herself up to sit beside him, "Right, totally fine. I might not speak your language, but I definitely recognize when someone is moping."

The prince sighed, "I do not wish to trouble you with my worries."

Alex stared at the surrounding field that masked their camp. Tall stalks of corn, or something similar.

Alex asked, "Why were you so far from the capital?"

The prince looked at her, his expression drooping even more.

"A diplomatic visit, one I felt unnecessary, but was insisted on by the court. The so-called country that I visited is hostile to ours. Very hostile, I was told directly that their leader wished a speedy death for my father."

Alex winced, "Yikes, that's harsh."

"There were two more guards with us when we set out. They did not make it home. You have witnessed two of five attempts at my life, and those are simply the ones that happened during this journey," said Calseous.

"Why do people want you dead?"

"I do not know, truly. I have done nothing, made no major impact, I have little power in the kingdom at all. My only true station is as an heir to my father's throne. But Father grows more ill by the day; his time is short."

"Fraygor said that the court was behind your guard's betrayal. You don't believe him?"

The prince turned to Alex, "I cannot! It is not in my nature to be so distrustful. Perhaps that is the place of people such as yourself, but I must believe that those who serve my kingdom are not killers and traitors."

Alex felt a pang of pity; he truly was naive. Not in a way that was endearing or enviable, just sad. "You really don't understand how the world works, do you?"

"If I may, Miss, you are not of this world, how would you know how it works?"

Alex supposed he had a point, but people were people and she had heard this story a thousand times. "Your court wants power, or at least that's how it sounds to me. If they take you out of the picture, they run the whole show."

"You are just as cynical as Fraygor!"

Alex shook her head, deciding to not take that personally, "I meant to ask, your scholars, do you think they'll be able to help us?"

"Oh yes, I have a plan," Calseous grinned.

"Yeah?"

"I shall take your case to the court. Many of the scholars are on the court, so to bring your case to them would be the most direct and honest way to get help."

Alex was confused, as clueless as the prince was, surely he couldn't believe that the people trying to kill him would help the strangers that thwarted their own assassination attempts. Before she could push back, Darius emerged from his tent, yawning loudly.

"Good morning, Alex."

Alex jumped down from the wagon, "Morning, Darius, sleep well?"

"Well enough."

Fraygor suddenly emerged from the field, "I've scouted ahead, no ambushes that I can see. We should be safe to move."

Alex asked, "About that, how are we going to move your wagon? Didn't those assassin guys kill your horses?"

Fraygor furrowed his brow, "Indeed…I don't suppose your metal carts can hold us all?"

Alex did the math in her head—two vehicles, five cramped seats each, that was ten seats for eleven people. "Sadly, no. Unless one of you wants to ride on the roof."

Charlie, or at least her hand, shot from her tent. With a single finger pointed upwards she said, "I have an idea!"

Minutes later everyone was awake, apart from the injured guards who lay only half-conscious in the prince's wagon. The team had tied up the antiquated transports to their own modern ones, in order to tow them behind the ATV's. Alex felt it was still the best plan even though it would certainly slow them down.

Their own supplies had been tightly stuffed into their small transports, and although slower, the wagons could carry much more. Leaving the prince's caravan worth of food would have been a loss as well. As they departed, Fraygor showed Alex a map. She figured it wouldn't take them more than two days to make it there at this speed.

CHAPTER 17

PERPLEXED, Fraygor and Alex studied a huge boulder that blocked their passage.

Curiously, neatly stacked smaller rocks surrounded the boulder.

"I do not believe for one moment that this is a natural rock-slide," Fraygor grumbled.

Alex nodded, "On that we agree."

Alex was anticipating another attack, but she didn't expect the prince's enemies would resort to sneakier tactics.

Alex looked back to the makeshift convoy, "Charlie!"

"Yeah?"

"Can you blow this rock up with the cannon?"

Charlie studied the boulder. She squinted and twisted her mouth, "I don't think that's gonna work, boss. We don't have much ammo for this thing, and there's no telling how much rock is behind the big one."

Alex sighed and looked at Fraygor, "I don't suppose there are other routes to take?"

Fraygor scowled and pulled out his map. "The quickest route is south, through the mountains. It's shorter, but difficult terrain. I trust your machines can handle it?"

Alex looked at the map. It wasn't anything like what she was used to. Obviously, they lacked the luxuries of satellite imagery, but the roads themselves were thoroughly detailed. She inspected it closely and noticed that there was another, albeit slightly longer road to the north.

"What about here?" she pointed to the alternate route.

"Caltesia is a large port town, critical to the kingdom's trade. The other route is safer. Protecting His Majesty through the town could be troublesome."

Alex figured that made sense if the rockslide had been natural, but if their enemies planned an ambush, surely the difficult terrain of the shorter route would be the logical choice. "Wouldn't they expect us to take the shorter route? And the mountains make a perfect place for an ambush."

Before Fraygor could respond, Calseous approached, "Have I heard you correctly? We journey to Caltesia? Splendid! They are celebrating the Festival of Flight at this time of year, if memory serves."

Fraygor sighed. He turned to the prince, then to Alex. "Yes, my liege, that is the plan."

"Fantastic! I have not been to an airship race since I was a child," Calseous practically skipped away, his joy evident.

Fraygor rolled his eyes at Alex and stowed his map. "It will be very difficult to make it through town with a low profile using your metal carriages. Do you have any ideas?"

Alex knew this problem would come up at some point, she just hoped it wouldn't be until they arrived at the capital. She looked at Fraygor and pursed her lips, "What exactly does Caltesia import?"

Fraygor looked at her curiously, "Well, first and foremost, magic."

"Magic?"

"Yes, magic. Magic items, knowledge of magic, practices of magic. Caltesia is the only readily available port for long distance travel into the Kingdom of Kestalia and the surrounding regions. People come from across the world."

Alex was still a bit skeptical about all the talk she had heard of magic, honest to goodness wizardry or whatever. Still, if the locals were used to fantastical things, maybe the horseless carriages weren't so out of place?

"Can magic pull a cart? Maybe we can use that as a cover."

"Yes, I've seen such things. But never made of metal as yours are."

Alex looked at the vehicles, and then the two wooden carts they towed.

"Who said they had to be metal?"

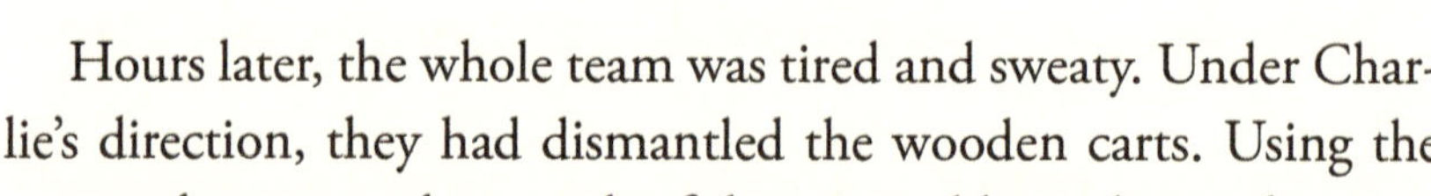

Hours later, the whole team was tired and sweaty. Under Charlie's direction, they had dismantled the wooden carts. Using the scraps, they covered as much of the exposed buggy's metal as possible, they even covered the cannon on the rear one.

While it had been Alex's idea, she knew that it wouldn't have been possible without Charlie's engineering background. She seemed to have instantly come up with a mental blueprint to make it work. Not only that, but it didn't look half bad.

Alex had pictured a shabby patchwork of wooden planks, but instead she was looking at a pair of nice wooden carriages. The offroad tires poked out from the bottom. Well, it was never going to be perfect.

"I will not lie, Alex, I am quite impressed," Fraygor smirked.

"You and me, both."

The previous problem of seating had been solved with the makeover, the front buggy now sporting two short benches on the sides, all in-line with the cart's aesthetic. The biggest benefit was the fact that they could now move much faster, no longer awkwardly towing the carriages. They could make it to the port before dark.

As they began mounting up, Alex noticed that Calseous seemed to be the only one disappointed with the outcome.

"My carriage..." he said glumly.

Alex smirked, "Come on your majesty, you're in here with us," she motioned to the lead buggy. They had rearranged the seating; the rear vehicle stayed the same, Charlie, Anthony, and Alicia. Now on the front vehicle, Isaac and Fraygor on the benches, ready to dismount at the first sight of trouble. Darius drove, with Alex next to him.

To his quiet but noticeable chagrin, the prince sat between his two unconscious guards who had been wounded in the attack. One thing Alex knew about medifoam, it totally knocked you out.

For several hours they navigated the roads, using Fraygor's map. Alex still had her head buried in navigation when she heard Calseous.

"There it is!"

Alex looked up, stunned at what she saw.

CHAPTER 18

ALEX HAD TRAVELED THE WORLD, well her world at least. But she had never seen a sight like this.

Brilliant bright blue sea spread out into the horizon. Half of the city of Caltesia seemed to be the water. Dozens and dozens of buildings—were they floating? Or were they somehow anchored under the water?

The architecture was strikingly different from Kresgroh, instead of stone houses, these were ornate and magnificent structures made of wood. Some larger buildings seemed to be made from sailing ships. One roof appeared to be an inverted galleon.

A dozen or so crafts painted a dizzying array of colors and patterns, lined up, zipping above the water, passing each other.

Maybe some sort of race?

Alex was fascinated.

Calseous jumped to his feet. "The races! They've begun!"

"Woah." Darius brought the convoy to a halt, and they all marveled at the spectacle of it all.

"Let's…keep moving, Darius. I get the feeling we'll be seeing a lot more," Alex shook her head at the prince's giddy expression.

Smells of spices and sea spray filled the air as they descended a steep hill down into the outskirts of the city. More ornate when viewed from up close, complex engravings adorned the sides of the buildings.

The wooden road creaked beneath the weight of their vehicles as they passed over it, and the water sloshed between the planks. The crowds were far larger than Kresgroh, but more orderly. They seemed to have 'lanes' formed, with carts and wagons each going one direction in the center of the road, and wooden paths for the pedestrians on either side. It was remarkably more structured than the hamlet atmosphere they had experienced up to this point. Everyone seemed to know where to go, in a very efficient manner, and how to avoid everyone else while doing so. This was especially impressive, because the town did not seem to be built with any sort of plan. It was, both from a distance and up close, a patchwork of slapped together, beautiful structures but many overlapped haphazardly.

Alex was happy she and her team didn't seem to stick out as much as she had worried. People paid them no mind, apart from impatience from other wagon drivers who seemed to feel Darius was moving too slow.

"I guess horseless carriages are on the lower end of interesting things in this place," said Alex.

The town, however, was conspicuous to the team. On either side of the road, beyond the lanes of people walking, were shops, sales yards, warehouses, and all manner of items for sale. It seemed nothing was off-limits, with everything from potions to creatures on display.

A man with pointed ears was peddling animals performing little circus tricks, juggling and balancing on beams. One hollering saleswoman tried to convince the passersby that her potions could improve their vision. Magic was no longer in doubt either, people conjured light out of the air, spinning fireballs in their hands in a street performance, even levitating above the ground.

They had gone from a simple forest and field road into the thick of another culture—one Alex had virtually no reference for. Sounds of bartering, argument, conversation, and expressions of awe surrounded them.

Alex said, "Darius, remind me—"

A loud screeching cry rose and fell as a whoosh rocked the transport when an airship passed overhead with great speed. A large, winged creature dragged it through the air.

Alex continued, "Remind me…to scrub 'simple medieval society,' from my reports…"

"The bazaar is as lively as ever," Calseous said, a hint of pride in his voice.

Alex leaned out of a narrow window to make sure Isaac was still there. He was. Given how quickly he had run off after seeing shiny swords in Kresgroh, she was almost certain she would lose him at some point in *this* place.

The radio crackled to life and Charlie's voice came through, *"Boss, are you seeing this?"*

"Yeah, Charlie, I'm seeing it. Not believing it, but I *am* seeing it."

"Alicia is practically drooling!" Charlie laughed. If they hadn't been in such a serious situation, Alex might be almost as excited as the others.

But still digging its way back into her thoughts was the fear of never going home, of letting down everyone back at the outpost. She dismissed it from her mind.

After a few more minutes of slowly rolling through town, Darius said, "We're about to hit a fork here Alex, what way do we turn?"

Alex looked at the map, but it only showed the roads *leading* to town, not the roads within the town.

"Uhh, I have no idea. We need Fraygor."

"I can tell you where to go, Miss Alex!" Calseous grabbed the map straight from Alex's hands.

"Hey!"

"We shall turn *right,* Mister Darius."

Darius looked at Alex, as if for confirmation.

She shrugged. The roads had been continually winding and

Alex had no clue what direction they were going, or how far into town they were. "I guess. He's at least been here before, that's more than I can say for either of us."

Darius turned right onto an even busier and more crowded road, and their pace slowed.

The prince excitedly pointed to the side of the road, "Oh! Oh, stop here, Mister Darius!"

Alex looked around, "What? Why?" But the transport had already stopped, and the prince was quickly out the door.

Alex jumped out of the buggy, "Dangit," she growled.

Fraygor had already gone after the prince.

Isaac seemed confused and stayed on the bench. "Are we stopping, boss?"

The other cart pulled in behind them. "Not sure *why,* but apparently yes." Darius pulled to the side of the road, and she was relieved they weren't blocking the traffic. No longer in the cramped confines of the buggy, Alex took in the sensations of the town.

Alex's adventurous nature would have her wandering the streets, but she couldn't risk the prince running off. Everything relied on him.

She followed Fraygor through the crowds, and as they got closer to the water she heard cheering growing louder as they neared.

Eventually, she reached a sort of railing, a barrier to prevent people from falling into the sea. Dozens upon dozens of people leaned against the rail watching the sky over the bay. Those colorful darting shapes they had seen when they entered the town were much closer now. Scaly flying creatures dragged the airships through the sky. As the prince had said, they were lined up and seemed to be racing. Floating pillars suspended in the air apparently designated some sort of course.

From at least a dozen people away, Calseous shouted, "Miss Alex! Fantastic, isn't it?"

The idiot.

Trudging over to him, she found the prince with Fraygor, who was at least inconspicuous and not nearly as engrossed in the race as the prince was.

Alex glared at the two, "What part of 'low-profile' do you not understand? We're not here to see the sights, we're supposed to be passing through quietly."

Alex was mad, but the sight really was spectacular and one that piqued her interest given her background in flying. She found it hard to look away, even as she scolded the prince for doing the same.

"Oh, come now, Miss Alex," said Calseuos. "Surely racing through town without stopping to see the main attraction would be more noticeable? We must engage in the culture! Although I must say the view here is not nearly as good as the seats in the royal perch…"

Great, now he was openly talking about being a royal. Alex was baffled by this guy's cluelessness. But maybe he had a point, if the assassins *were* planning on catching them in this city, they probably wouldn't expect them to stop and see the races.

Alex sighed, leaned against the railing, and watched the races. It didn't take long for her to become almost as engaged as Calseuos. Back home this would have been considered an unsafe sport, although she supposed it wasn't any more dangerous than most other races.

The ships would bump into each other, sometimes they'd lose altitude quickly and draw a collective gasp from the crowd, with cheers once they recovered. At one point, Alex noticed two ships, very close to each other, slow down as the beasts pulling them began to fight.

"What are those things pulling the airships?" Alex asked the prince, not taking her eyes off of the spectacle.

"Wyverns!" the prince said, "Fearsome creatures, quite strong, although rather stupid and horrible smelling."

Alex chuckled, "Why do you know so much about them? You don't seem like you get out very often."

"My scholars teach me much, Miss Alex, I especially love learning of the creatures of the world."

Fraygor placed a firm hand on the young prince's shoulder, "My lord, we really shouldn't linger…"

Calseuos sighed, "Very well, Fraygor, the race seems to be coming to a close anyway."

As the trio pushed through the crowds, Alex heard Charlie's voice shouting something. She couldn't understand her from here, but it was Charlie, and she was angry.

Alex quickened her pace and stepped past the last few people, only to find a standoff between her team and a group of heavily armored guards. They looked almost like stereotypical Medieval knights, although their pointed helmets had strange metal bat wings atop each of them.

A guard yelled, "Ma'am, step away from the wagon!" His armor was trimmed with a shinier, almost gold-looking metal, presumably to signify he was the leader of the group.

Charlie stood her ground with her arms spread wide, "No way, I'm not budging."

She glanced at Alex. "Boss! They were rooting through our stuff; they're trying to take the carts!"

The head guard marched towards Alex, leaving his subordinates with their polearms lowered to a ready position. They were prepared for a fight, and while Charlie and the others didn't have their weapons *drawn*, the situation was tense.

CHAPTER 19

"THIS WOMAN calls you her boss. Might I assume she is correct?"

"That she is, I'm Alexandria Petrakis. Who are you?"

The man raised his brow at her name. She wondered briefly if she should have used a fake one. Petrakis was Greek, which wasn't exactly local.

"I am Jundor Hef'krost. You may call me *Captain* Hef'krost."

"Captain, what exactly is the problem?"

"We have reason to believe you have stolen these carts. They are very obviously magical items and yet none from your group seem to be mages. There are two wounded and unconscious people in one of the carts, and your compatriots interfered with our search of the vehicles. Surely, it is obvious this is all suspicious behavior."

Alex looked past the captain, and sure enough the rear doors of the cart were open and some of the items spread out on the ground.

"Furthermore, before our search was interrupted we found a number of seemingly magical artifacts, foreign objects as well as a great deal of fine food. Given your rather plain clothing, we have concluded you have purloined these goods. We request that you quietly come with us to investigate this," said Captain Hef'krost.

Alex looked for Fraygor, but neither he nor the prince were anywhere to be seen.

"Dangit."

They were her easiest way out of this mess.

"Captain Hef'krost, I promise we're not thieves, we're just… not from around here." She wasn't sure how to lie in a way that would end well. "My friends and I are not mages, true, but we are transporting these goods to the capital. I apologize for their defensiveness; we've been attacked since we entered your kingdom."

"I see, well if you are transporting these items legally, then I am sure you will have a writ of commerce?" The captain raised a brow.

"A what?"

Now the man furrowed his brow, "A writ, an official record of your entry to the port and the goods that you carry. It is required for all legitimate trade passing through Caltesia."

Of all the things that she had expected to cause them trouble in this swords and sorcery magical land they found themselves in, not once had Alex anticipated paperwork.

"No sir, as I said we are from a far-off land and are unfamiliar with your trade laws. If you might direct us to where we could obtain one—"

The man suddenly turned his attention back to his guards. "Seize the carts!"

With a collective shout, the guards all lowered their polearms, each now squarely aimed at the team.

Alex's team drew their own weapons Multiple cracks, from a stun-gun firing. The prongs harmlessly plinked off of the thick metal armor they wore with a 'ding'.

Alex rushed forward to help but was blocked by the plate-mail-clad arm of the captain. She struggled to get past and shouted to her team, "Shells! Non-lethal!" She spun on the captain. "This is a mistake," she hissed.

"I assure you that you are correct, *you* have made a mistake," he swung his free arm at Alex.

She ducked, avoiding the strike, and rolled to the side. With space between them, she had time to think.

The armor he wore, although ornate, was still very practical. She didn't think she could do much with her bare hands, so she reached for her holster, but saw it on the ground with the straps cut.

Hef'krost was more clever than she had given him credit for; she hadn't even realized he disarmed her. Her team was loading one-shot shells in their sidearms. Each of the rubber projectiles had to be manually loaded, but they came in a wide variety of types that had endless utility.

Confident with her team, and hearing the stomps of encroaching boots, she turned her attention back to her own fight.

The captain, armed with a massive longsword, moved towards her with the blade raised over his shoulder, the tip still pointed at her. This wasn't like the rough swings from the orcs she had dealt with, this man was trained martially. Luckily, all that armor made him a lot less dexterous compared to her.

Alex tucked to the side away from his slash, and curled her leg, aiming a swift kick at the biggest gap in the armor she could see. With a heavy combat boot digging in between the plates that covered his thigh and torso, Hef'krost stumbled to one knee, his sword scraping against the ground.

Alex dove for her holster, using a free hand to snag a shell off the strap and slid it into the chamber. She turned on her attacker, who planted his sword in the ground to raise himself up.

With a snarl he charged, his heavy blade scraping along the ground. Alex fired, a heavy crack piercing her ears.

A large dent appeared in the polished metal of the armor on the guard captain's right shoulder, and he dropped his heavy weapon.

"What magic is this? You've not casted a thing!" he winced and spat through gritted teeth. Alex heard more cracks, her team opening fire almost in unison., Alex smirked and then glared at the heavily armored man ahead of her. "You don't want this fight,

Captain, we're just trying to pass through."

"I do not look the other way for criminals, no matter their tricks!" he grunted and lumbered towards her.

"STOP!" Calseous discarded his cloak leaving only his 'princely' attire. "I demand you cease! So says the Prince of Kestalia!"

Alex scoffed. The last thing she needed right now was to have to protect his highness again.

Suddenly, she heard the clack of metal touching stone. The captain knelt before the prince, his arms in that same peculiar salute. A chorus of similar sounds erupted from behind her as the remaining guards followed their leader's example.

All right, that was unexpected.

Fraygor followed the prince.

"Stand, Captain, we've not the time for ceremony," said Fraygor.

"My Liege," said Hef'krost. "What issue do you take with our dispensation of justice?"

"These people are escorting me to the capitol. There is no need for such brutish violence," Calseous was more serious than Alex was used to.

The captain turned to Alex, and she nodded.

"Men, back on patrol. I'll deal with this," Hef'krost bellowed..

The guards dispersed, and her own team cautiously holstered their weapons. Alex was proud of how her friends had handled themselves, they protected each other *and* the mission, without flinching.

Hef'krost asked, "What brings you to Caltesia? We are not usually the most direct route to the capital."

"Just seeing the sights. I do love the races, you know," the prince lied.

"Listen, Captain, you're the first person who hasn't wanted to kill the prince since I first met him. Everyone else seems to want him dead," said Alex.

"Perhaps, this is not the most suitable place to discuss such things," Fraygor whispered, his distrustful eyes monitoring the crowd that had gathered to watch the fight.

"Agreed. Come with me," Hef'krost struck a markedly friendlier tone.

CHAPTER 20

ALEX GRIMACED as the sweet scent of the bazaar transitioned into the bitter mixtures and concoctions of the tavern. She wasn't an expert in alcohol, but she could tell they weren't just serving drinks but also brewing them somewhere in the building. The sour scent of fermentation wafted between the barstools as the raucous pageantry of the outside was replaced by a quiet and unassuming atmosphere of the tavern's interior.

Hef'krost led them to a quiet booth in the back corner, where many of the patrons wore similar outfits to the 'gambeson' worn under Hef'krost's own armor. With those folks all grouped up at tables, and few other patrons besides them, Alex assumed rather quickly that they must be in the local equivalent of a cop bar back home. She had spent enough time with her grandpa to know the atmosphere of one of those places, and while it wasn't a direct comparison, clearly some cultural things translated between worlds.

Most of the team stayed behind to tend to the carts. Alex initially invited Alicia, but Fraygor insisted that it would be easier to quietly move around with fewer people. Still, Alex was happy that Alicia seemed to be doing better since they entered Caltesia.

She was best in her element of researching other cultures. This must have been exactly what she was looking forward to when she signed on for this expedition.

As the group settled into the booth, Hef'krost ordered them something, the names of the foods,...or drinks didn't translate. She wasn't sure which was which.

The situation still seemed tense to Alex.

Although the fight had ended without any real injuries, it was still a fight, and a jarring transition to now sharing a meal. At the back of her mind as well, Alex was apprehensive about the drinks themselves. Alcohol had been an issue in her family historically, so she steered clear of it her whole life. How would she avoid it now in this delicate situation? And worse, how strong was the stuff from not only a city from another world, and a *magic* city at that?

Fraygor broke the uneasy silence by addressing Hef'krost, "It's been quite some time since I've been here. I am glad to see this place is still around."

Hef'krost chuckled, "Yes, I don't think Hyetcar will ever let this place go, nor would his kids for that matter."

Alex saw Fraygor crack the first genuine smile she had seen from the man. The tense situation eased, at least it seemed to her.

Hef'krost asked Fraygor, "What then truly does bring you here? Your friend speaks of the prince as though he is a target."

Fraygor's eyes darted to Alex, notable frustration behind his tired gaze.

"Unfortunately, she is mostly correct. Calseous has had multiple attempts on his life since we left the capital, especially on the way back."

Alex noted the informal way Fraygor talked about the prince, a clear departure from what she was used to. Prince Calseous sat sheepishly in the corner. He seemed even less accustomed to the situation than Alex was.

"Has the situation in the capital grown that dire?" asked Hef'krost.

"I'm afraid it's worse than you might think. Lord Arathos is on his deathbed, and each member of the court is eager to seize power for themselves. I would not be shocked if the assassins we have encountered were sent by many different parties," Fraygor admitted.

"What's worse is that one of your own people was one of them," Alex said flatly.

Fraygor grimaced at the mention, "Yes, that is also true."

Hef'krost's expression turned sullen, "Then, it truly is worse than I thought. The kingdom always seems to maintain a certain level of dramatics."

"Captain, I understand that you are in a delicate situation, but you must agree that Caltesia's future is in the balance," said Fraygor.

"Why is that?" asked Alex.

Hef'krost turned his attention to her, closed his eyes, and let out a heavy sigh.

"I'm afraid that those in the court all disagree with one another on the issue of our city's bid for independence. The only one truly in favor of it is the king. When he dies, our fate lies in the murky uncertainty of squabbling politicians."

Alex had heard that story before, back on earth. "So, it's in your interest to protect Calseous, right?"

"It is not that simple, Alex," said Fraygor. "Captain Hef'krost aiding the prince openly could be seen as Caltesia taking a side in the court's power struggle. Whatever chance at independence they have could be swept away."

Alex was beginning to understand what Fraygor had said earlier about dueling loyalties. This was beginning to feel a lot less straightforward than her initial plan.

She turned to the prince. "Well, What if you didn't do it so openly? As far as anyone in town knows, all you've done so far is stop the prince's convoy and take him and his head guard away, right? The people trying to kill him wouldn't have a problem with that."

Fraygor and Hef'krost exchanged a brief glance before Hef'krost asked, "What are you proposing?"

Alex looked in the Captain's eyes and laid out her plan. "We have two of his guards. They need some rest, but they'll be awake soon, and we don't have much room for them. Station them outside of your headquarters, or wherever the guards would take him. Make the assassins think that's where the prince is. We'll sneak him away, and you'll know exactly where they are so you can fight them on your own terms."

Hef'krost raised a bushy eyebrow, "Decoys for an ambush? With no retribution from the court, the benefactors of the assassins would show themselves. I must say Miss, I truly am glad I did not defeat you earlier."

Alex smirked, "So am I."

Hef'krost chuckled, "Fraygor, where did you find this one?"

Fraygor cracked another smile, "I'm not sure you would believe me if I told you."

Alex returned a coy smile; she was beginning to like the old bodyguard.

"Fine then," said Hef'krost. "Keep your secrets, old man."

As the two men continued talking, Alex noticed that Calseous looked incredibly uncomfortable.

Perhaps, it was the casual conversation about his life being at stake, or the seemingly impending death of his father. It certainly wasn't helping that both guardsmen had been speaking about him as though he wasn't in the room.

Alex hadn't been much better in that regard. She leaned over to the prince, who was sitting next to her.

"Calseous," she whispered.

"Prince Calseous."

Alex sighed, "Right. Whatever, are you okay?"

Calseous, who had been looking at the table this entire time, barely lifting his eyes to her. "This is not quite my element, Miss Alex."

"Just Alex."

"Oh whatever," the prince sounded defeated. "I am not suited for tavern booths and talk of sneaky ambushes. Who knows what could happen next? What if a drunkard walks past us, or worse, starts one of those 'brawls' I hear about so often in places such as these."

Alex stifled a chuckle, "Are you really more worried about that than assassins?"

The prince looked at her but said nothing.

Right, probably not helping.

"Listen, Calseous," she said. "I'm sorry we're talking about this like it's not a big deal, but we are all trying to protect you."

Calseous looked at her, though he barely moved his head. "Alex, I've been protected my entire life, I've never once been hurt, but I've been listened to just as rarely."

Alex was confused.

"The title of prince alone grants me only the station of an honorary court member. Upon the king's death, the fate of my station relies on the court."

"What? You don't just *become* king?"

"Kestalia is not strictly ruled by bloodline, the court must determine the suitability of the king or queen's successor. If they are determined to be unsuitable by the court nobles, then they are cast out of the castle and left as an average citizen."

The situation was much more complicated than Alex first thought.

"Why would they not find you suitable? The ones that aren't trying to kill you I mean."

The prince chuckled but only briefly, "I intend to promote a system of self-ruling, wherein the people will decide who is on the court, rather than the court themselves nominating and voting the members in," he said proudly.

"You mean democracy?" asked Alex.

Now Calseous was confused. "I know not what that word means."

Right, Greek.

"It's a 'my world' word for what you're talking about. It's actually a very common practice where I'm from," said Alex.

His eyes widened. "That is splendid to hear. It is a poorly kept secret that this is my intention, and few in the court are supportive of it. They argue that the people love the court the way it is, so why change anything."

"If the people love them so much then surely they'd elect them right back onto the court. The only ones that should be worried are the ones the people don't like, what else is there to fear?" Alex said.

Calseous' expression returned to one of uncertainty. "That is the problem. For so long as the court functioned this way, most of those that are on the court are there by bloodline. They nominate one another and their kin in expansive and fragile alliances. It is unpredictable at times, violent even. I wish to be free of it."

"Sounds like a mess," Alex leaned back in the booth.

"Indeed."

"Gotta say your highness, this seems to be at odds with your previous assessment that the members of the court can't be traitors or killers," Alex looked around the tavern.

"I cannot believe that they would kill me, even if it is true. I believe in my kingdom Miss Alex, if it's run by vile loathsome murderers, then what is there to believe in?"

Alex didn't have a quick answer, and before she could even give it much thought she heard Hef'krost calling her name.

He stood, "Alex! I like your plan, and I think I know the perfect way to execute it. It will take some time to arrange, but you will travel in the dwarven underground."

Alex stared at him,"Dwarves? Like short, bearded people?"

"Ah, so you know of them!" Hef'krost's face lit up.

Alex sighed; this was going to be a long day.

CHAPTER 21

As THEY RETURNED to their transports, Alex was surprised to find her teammates having polite conversation with a few of the guards they had been fighting a couple of hours ago. Darius engaged in boisterous laughter with three of the guards. Isaac appeared to be inspecting a guard's armor.

Charlie and Alicia talked with other guards. Charlie showing off her rifle to one and Alicia vigorously taking notes as another talked. Alex watched the exchange of cultures and technologies, and wondered if standing out might not be a bad thing. After all, their mission wasn't to explore in secret anymore, it was to get home, so getting better acquainted might be worth doing.

She walked up to Darius, "Sorry to interrupt Darius, but we have a new plan."

Darius hoisted himself up from the crate he had been using as a makeshift seat. "How'd things go with the guard captain? Hopefully as well as things are going here."

"Better actually, he's going to help us get out of the city undetected, but he needs a day or two to arrange it," said Alex.

Isaac startled Alex, "I think we can hide out in this city for another day. I certainly wouldn't mind seeing more of it."

The real question is, how do we blend in without putting ourselves in the open too much? I'm not sure standing out would be such a great idea so long as the assassins were an issue.

"Miss Alex, if I may," Calseous said timidly, "The city is only as lively as it is because of the races. As I said earlier, I believe it would be more conspicuous if we were not attending them."

Alex couldn't argue with that, not entirely at least. Her eyes wandered again to the airships darting across the bay. She'd be lying if she said the pilot in her wasn't intrigued by the prospect of otherworldly aviation.

"Well, I guess you have a point. What was that you said earlier about the 'royal perch'?"

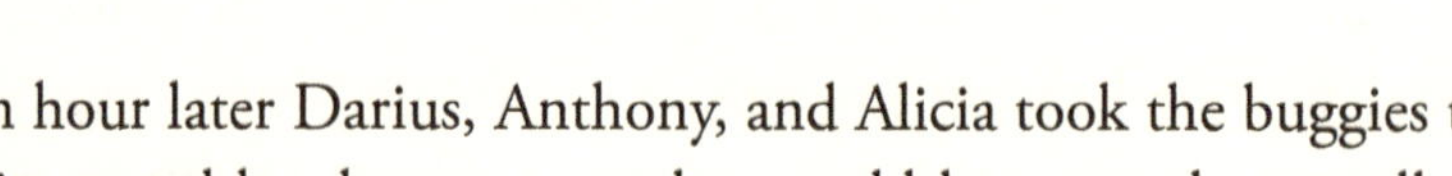

An hour later Darius, Anthony, and Alicia took the buggies to the city guard headquarters so they could keep watch over all of their equipment.

With Charlie and Isaac in tow, Alex followed Fraygor and Calseous along the docks on the bayside part of town.

Calseous was taking them to the 'Royal Perch' as he called it. The inconsistent yet frequent creaks of the planks slightly unnerved Alex; she wasn't big on water. She was surprised when the sun was blotted out as they rounded a corner, heading away from the sea.

Ahead was a towering structure, easily hundreds of feet tall, with dozens of ropes anchoring it to the various nearby buildings. Its size, however, was of secondary interest. It was apparent to Alex that the 'structure' was in-fact an entire sail ship, a frigate, or some other large vessel. Its bow, the front of the ship, was buried in the ground, piercing the deck of the city's expansive pier. The tail end of the ship formed the peak, a large opening in what would most likely have been the officer's quarters. The masts, abnormally long, had been converted to long docks, with several of the racing airships moored to them.

The prince beamed with pride. “Magnificent, is it not?”

The team gawked at the bizarre building and Alex didn’t take her eyes from the spectacle when she said, “I’m guessing there’s a story behind this?”

“Oh, ooh, Fraygor, do tell the story, you tell it so much better than I,” said the giddy Prince.

Fraygor took a deep breath. “It belonged to the Imperial navy of the nation that used to rule these lands hundreds of years ago. One day the Imperial fleet came home to find the Empire had collapsed, so they decided to settle this area and live out their days as peaceful traders. They used every ship of what was once one of the largest navies in the known world to construct this city, this tower was their flagship, the ‘Caltesia’, for which the city is named.”

“I love this world,” Isaac said, almost drooling.

Fraygor grinned and continued. “This is where the racers dock their ships. Many years ago, the royal perch was constructed at the top, so that royalty and other important figures could have the best view of the whole event. Let’s head up.”

They followed Calseous; Alex looked up at the airships. They were not anything like the airships back on earth, rather they looked like small olde-timey sailing ships. Their envelope, the balloon holding them aloft, was puffy and uneven, and their hulls were sleek, almost aerodynamic. These were clearly built for speed. She noticed Charlie was just as interested.

“How do you think they steer ‘em?” she asked.

Alex guessed, “Probably a combination of control surfaces and those weird dragon things the prince mentioned.”

“Dragons? Oh no, no, no,” the prince interjected, “Wyverns. Those beasts are called wyverns. Dragons are far larger and smarter.”

They ascended a large spiral staircase and Alex saw Fraygor looking over his shoulder now and again. It was obvious he was protective of the prince, but Alex wasn’t sure if it was duty, loyalty, or respect.

Hoping for any reprieve she could get at this point, Alex had let her guard down, opting to take in the city a bit more. If she stayed on edge all the way to the capital she would probably go insane. She couldn't see any way that the prince's would-be killers could make it into something called 'the royal perch'.

That was her hope at least.

Reaching the top of the lengthy staircase, the group was greeted with a cozy lounge. There was a bar, and all manner of seats and sofas. Alex chuckled as she mentally compared it to a medieval hotel lobby. What made it different however, was the expansive, crystal-clear window, perfectly positioned to look out over the bay. It was flanked on either side by slimmer stained-glass panes, ornate designs depicting the races in bright colors.

Alex could see the airship dock clearly from their elevated position. It seemed many of the racing ships were being repaired, some even modified. At the end of the docks was a pen filled with those 'Wyvern' creatures. With only a high fence with a thick netting covering the top, Alex felt like that wasn't the most secure. But then she didn't know anything about wyverns.

Alex asked, "Are the races done for the day?"

Calseous nodded, "The true ones, yes. There is a rather informal one that takes place at night. It is primarily to show off a display of dazzling lights."

"Have you always been so interested in the races?"

The prince's expression turned somber, "I attended the races every year as a child, with my father and mother."

It was only at that moment that Alex realized she had never heard Calseous mention his mother.

He continued, "It was one of the only times of year that we would all be together, our holiday away from the hustle and bustle of the capital."

Alex didn't want to interrupt his musing, but the wistful look in his eyes betrayed her judgment. "Calseous, if you don't mind me asking, what happened to your mom?"

His shoulders slumped slightly, and he closed his eyes. "She simply was no longer here one day. She was very outspoken against the court, even taking on direct threats from them. Truly a fearless woman." He looked directly into her eyes, "You quite remind me of her Miss Alex."

Alex smiled, that might have been the first meaningful compliment he had given her, and he had a way of conveying the respect that came with it.

"You never found out what happened to her?"

"The assumption to this day is that she—how would Fraygor put it, disappeared? Either kidnapped and taken into hiding or worse, killed and...disposed of."

The way he spoke of it, almost casually, carried a numb acceptance of the situation.

"But whatever the case, she will remain forever gone, I fear." He blinked and turned to face the window.

Alex looked past Calseous, to Fraygor, who was giving her a slight glare, seemingly upset she had brought any of this up.

Maybe Calseous' life hadn't been as cushy as Alex had assumed, it sounded like things were largely out of his control, something she herself knew would drive her crazy. Sometimes Alex had a hard time connecting with other people, and part of that was because she often forgot that everyone else had their own struggles.

Her conversation with her team, hearing about their lives, their fears, and scars, had really brought things into perspective for her. She looked at Charlie and Isaac, both of whom were staring out the window in amazement. Happy as they were now, they had also struggled at times in their lives.

She turned back to the prince, "Calseous, that night in the woods—"

A woosh, loud boom, and spray of glass shards in every direction; the window shattered.

Alex covered her head and with one arm shielding her face, she looked around for the source of the commotion.

At the entrance to the lounge stood five robed figures wearing strange masks. The one in front of the group had his hand extended, a faint blue glow coming from within it.

Charlie shouted, "*More* assassins?!"

The other attacker's hands had the same blue glow, and bolts of energy shot from them. Alex's group narrowly evaded a volley when they all ducked to the ground.

"*Magic* assassins!" Isaac yelled.

Fraygor leapt forth and flipped one of the room's large dining tables onto its side. "Get behind!"

Once everyone had joined him in the makeshift cover, Alex, Charlie, and Isaac drew their pistols. Alex peaked out of the cover and took a shot at the group, but as soon as she pulled the trigger, a glowing green triangle appeared in front of the attackers. Alex's shot impacted the strange barrier, a ripple dancing across it before it flickered and faded away.

She ducked back down, "Oh yeah Charlie, we'll win every fight, they'll just have dinky swords."

"How was I supposed to know there would be magic wizards with lightning fingers?!" The words tumbled out of Charlie's mouth.

"Doesn't matter. We need a way out of here,"

At that very moment she saw an airship from the race passing by the window. It was close enough, at least she hoped so. She tried to gauge the distance, "I have a plan, I just hope it's not a dumb one."

"That is not even remotely reassuring!" The prince shouted as more of the magical bolts whizzed past them.

One impacted the table, splintering the wood and breaking open a hole in their cover.

"I don't think we have much of a choice right now," Alex said, hoisting herself from her crouched position.

"Come on!" She broke into a sprint and, in the biggest leap of her life, jumped the gap from the broken window to the passing airship. She winced when her body collided with

the hard wooden planks, and she rolled across the deck.

Isaac, then Charlie, followed right behind her and landed almost simultaneously; narrowly reaching the deck of the ship.

Alex pulled herself up just as Calseous leaped and landed in a heap on the deck.

Ready to jump, Fraygor was struck with an assassin's projectile propelling him out the window towards them. He didn't make it to the deck but latched onto the edge. Isaac leaped forward grabbing Fraygor's arm, both men groaning as Isaac strained to get him to safety.

"Charlie!" Alex shouted.

Charlie rushed to help the two men.

Alex ran to the helm, shoved the bewildered sailor out of the way. "Sorry guy, I'm sure you're good at your racing thing but I don't think you're used to being shot at."

The bewildered sailor ran away from her.

Alex gripped the old-fashioned pirate ship wheel, but it didn't respond as she expected. It looked like any helm she had seen in any number of movies, but when she tilted the wheel the ship rocked side to side, throwing everyone onto the deck.

"Sorry!"

"Get us out of here!" yelled Fraygor.

Aware that Charlie and Isaac were firing back at their attackers, she tried to figure out how to fly what was basically a medieval blimp.

Suddenly, she saw a handle dangling from the balloon. She yanked it downwards, but to no effect. She glanced around and noticed the wyvern perched on the mast of the ship. Following a hunch, she let go of the handle, and it shot back up to its original position, with a loud 'crack', much like a spring-loaded whip.

The beast suddenly shrieked and took flight, lurching the ship forward; it was tugged along by the serpentine creature.

Stop and go, got it.

She moved the helm back and forth, rocking the ship and causing it to bank slightly.

Roll.

Finally, she turned the wheel to the left and steered the ship away from the perch.

Yaw—okay.

"Alex you got this," she took a deep breath and tried to focus.

Cranking the handle a few more times she picked up speed, and as they pulled away from their aggressors the projectiles became fewer and less accurate.

Charlie shouted, "Haha! See you later you stupid wizards!"

Alex laughed, breathing a sigh of relief as they got further away from danger. Her celebration was short-lived however when she saw a shadow pass over the deck. To her right were two approaching airships, just like this one.

They were out speeding her, and soon they had overtaken Alex's ship, positioning themselves on either side.

She expected them to fire more of their weird spell things, but instead she saw them turning in towards her.

They were ramming them!

The ship quaked as the other crafts intermittently bumped into the side, getting close enough that Alex could see the occupants were wearing those same strange masks. Their magical attacks resumed.

Charlie and Isaac tried in vain to hit their aggressors, but between the flurry of magical projectiles and the motion of the ship, there was no way they would hit anything.

Alex pulled the handle repeatedly but couldn't out speed them.

What sort of crumby racing ship had she gotten? Suddenly both ships flanking either side of her turned away, gaining a wide distance from her, before turning directly back in towards her.

Oh boy, this was gonna be a big one.

Her mind switched to her pilot's training. Suddenly she had a terrible, ridiculous, completely out-there idea. On instinct, she went into action. The maneuver was called a 'side-slip.'

Using both arms, she strained to quickly spin the wheel to the left, while leaning it in the opposite direction. As she did this, the ship rolled to the right, but its nose moved to the left, leaving the entire vessel flying forward with its side facing the direction it was traveling.

She was flying sideways, and as the airflow hit the broad side of the ship it pushed back, causing significant drag and rapidly slowing them down.

As they slipped backwards and out of danger, the two enemy ships collided with a mighty crash. Splintered wood flew everywhere, the ropes connecting the ships to their balloons broke free, and they quickly started going down.

She slowly eased off the controls and yanked the handle, bringing them to a complete stop as the ship jerked back into a normal position.

Alex heard a whoop behind her as Isaac cheered and ran towards her.

"That was amazing, boss! Way to go!"

Charlie ran up behind him. "I gotta say, I'm pretty impressed. Once a pilot, always a pilot."

Alex beamed, she hadn't flown a thing in two years, and now she was flying a completely foreign aircraft from another world. Before she could soak in the admiration, she saw Fraygor slumped back against the railing of the ship. He wasn't bleeding, but she could see a large scorch across his right shoulder.

"Guys," Alex pointed towards him. The others stopped talking and the three hurried to their injured comrade. He had a substantial burn on his back. It was a serious wound, but no blood. Whatever energy or magic they shot him with had cauterized the wound instantly. Fraygor gritted his teeth as Isaac, and Alex, each took one of his arms, hoisted him over their shoulders.

Fraygor cried out in agony.

Alex reached for her radio. "We need to get you to Anthony now. He has our medifoam."

CHAPTER 22

THEY TOOK FRAYGOR to the tavern, their only real hiding place. The prince's remaining bodyguards were stationed outside the guard outpost as a diversion, leaving the tavern the only other safe place in town.

Anthony examined Fraygor's injuries. "It's a good thing you got him here quickly, even with no immediate blood loss, that could have gotten a lot worse really fast."

"That being said," Anthony continued, "field-grade Medifoam doesn't fix broken bones, and I'm almost positive he's got a fracture in his shoulder. Once we're at our destination, I can inject him with the stronger stuff. We need somewhere clean and secure to perform that sort of operation though."

Anthony packed up his first-aid kit. Alex was glad he wasn't just a 'scientist' scientist.

His medical knowledge was probably comparable to a medical degree, although he lacked one officially.

"Let's keep him here while we wait for Hef'krost to arrange our exit." She turned to Anthony. "Can you stay and watch him?"

Anthony nodded, heading over to sit with his new patient.

"What about the rest of us, boss?" asked Isaac.

Alex wasn't sure. With narrowly avoiding another assassination attempt, letting the prince out of the tavern was out of the question. Staying hunkered down, was the only thing she could think of.

"Alex, if I may," said Darius. "What if we spread out? The guard station is already a diversion, but what if some of us headed out into the town, trying to be as obvious as possible."

"I don't follow," Alex raised an eyebrow. "How does being obvious help?"

"If they knew we were at the tavern they would have attacked us here instead of the races. I think by now they must know what we look like, so if we're out and about showing ourselves, that will spread *them* out even further."

"And keep them too busy to find Calseous at the tavern. That's smart Darius."

"Don't sound so surprised," Darius said, smiling his goofy smile.

"You guys have fun in the world's biggest crowd, I'm staying here. Had enough quality time with murder magicians for one day." Charlie grumbled, waving a hand over her shoulder as she faced away from them, busy working on a pile of tech.

Isaac perked up. "Does this mean we get to explore the town?"

"Yes, Isaac, have fun but stay close," Alex said with a slight smirk. Despite it being the plan anyway, she felt she needed to at least act like she was doing it for Isaac's benefit. The kid was just too eager.

Alex, with Isaac, Darius, and Alicia headed out into the city. Despite it being late in the afternoon, bordering on early evening, it was still as crowded as when they had first arrived. Shortly after they had walked far enough from the tavern to not draw suspicion to it, Alex found herself standing in the city's center.

If Kresgoh had a 'town square' this was closer to a county fair back on Earth. The planked ground in this part of town was more neatly arranged than the rest of the city, forming a circular pattern all around the pavilion. In the middle of it all, stood a large bronze statue of a group of sailors, a plaque adorning the base.

The text on it was, of course, complete gibberish to them.

All around the pavilion there were carts, tents, and makeshift stages. People selling food seemed to take up the majority, but there were also musical performances and a wide variety of merchandise. As they passed one cart in particular, Alex was struck by a strong, spicy aroma. The woman running the shop was stirring a massive pot of some sort of stew, it kind of looked to Alex like a mix between curry and jambalaya.

"You're on!" she heard Darius say behind her. She turned to see Darius and Isaac staring each other down.

'Guys? What's going on?"

"Spicy food contest, Mister Ross here thinks he can handle the heat better than me," Darius laughed.

"You don't stand a chance, big guy. My grandma was Korean and had a taste-bud issue so she spiced everything to death. We all had to suffer through it, I am a hardened spicy-food veteran," said Isaac.

Alex laughed out loud for the first time since they got here. "I didn't think people could take an eating contest so seriously."

Alicia crossed her arms with a sigh. "Despite their age, men are all just boys deep down, for some things at least."

There was a brief silence between the two women.

"So…wanna bet who will win?" Alex was still watching their banter.

Alicia grinned, "Oh, totally."

A few minutes later, a crowd gathered watching Darius and Isaac eat spoonfuls of the strong-smelling dishes the chef was whipping up. Alex, with Alicia's help, and the prince's gold, had arranged for the shop-owner to prepare multiple dishes for them, each spicier than the last. The results had her laughing more than anything in a long time. Isaac's face was red as a tomato. Darius on the other hand, was sweating bullets and coughing pretty frequently.

"Give it up, Lieutenant," Isaac said with a strained voice. "You know I'm gonna win. If we both keep going, we won't be very useful on the mission."

Darius squinted, and with a shaky hand he raised the spoon from his bowl. A hush fell over the crowd and Darius defiantly stuffed the utensil into his mouth. One of Darius' eyes twitched as he chewed, and when he swallowed he started coughing violently. His coughing fit put him off balance on the small stool and he tumbled backwards and fell off.

Darius' coughing slowed down, "I—yield," he rasped.

The crowd broke into a deafening cheer.

Isaac stood and raised his hands in the air. "Thank you, Grandma and your spicy Kimchi!" he shouted.

Alex reluctantly handed Alicia three pieces of the local currency, the thick wide coins making a satisfying jangling noise as they changed hands. More cheers and more jangling rang through the crowd.

Their initial goal of causing a scene had worked and Isaac helped Darius up off the ground.

"Next time," Darius said, huffing between words. "We're lifting weights."

The crowd slowly dispersed, and Alex scanned the mass of people. She thought she saw a flash of one of those strange masks their previous attackers had been wearing. She was convinced they wouldn't attack in a crowd, but she had been wrong about the perch, so she kept her guard up. The team wandered around town for a few more hours, stopping to ask questions and buy souvenirs. Once back at the tavern, Alex was relieved to see Fraygor sitting up no longer half-conscious. Calseous was asleep in one of the bar's booths, a blanket draped across him.

Anthony was sitting at the bar preoccupied with his tablet, and Alex took a seat next to him. "Any word from Hef'krost?"

"Not that I've heard, but everyone is here, except for the prince's other bodyguards."

"Did we get them set up at the guard post?"

"Yes, although they're still recovering from the effects of the medifoam, they won't put up much of a fight if the assassins do end up attacking there." Anthony shut off his tablet and stowed it in his bag. "It's not a great idea to put recovering patients like that in the line of fire, but I guess we don't really have any alternatives."

Alex knew he was right, on both counts. This was their best plan, and they didn't have time to come up with another one.

Darius passed by them. "We're heading to bed; I need to sleep off this spicy food headache."

Isaac smiled as he strutted past with a large, tacky, medallion for his trophy. Alex still couldn't believe they had convinced her to buy that, but as far as she was concerned it was the prince who bought it.

Alex turned back to Anthony, but before she could say anything she heard the door to the tavern swing open and Hef'krost walked directly to Alex.

"It's time! It took some arranging, but I've got you a pass into the underground," he beamed, "But you'll have to leave now the window they gave me is short."

Alex raised an eyebrow, "Who's they?"

He removed his helmet. "I'm afraid I cannot tell you; the dwarves are very secretive about these things."

"So…*they* meaning the dwarves?"

Hef'krost raised a finger but lowered it in defeat just as quickly.

"Your wits are as formidable as your fighting."

Alex stifled a laugh. Hef'krost was an odd combination of dutiful and airheaded, at least that's what she had gleaned during the few brief interactions she had had with him.

"Well, Anthony, you want to tell everyone they aren't sleeping tonight or shall I?" Alex turned to see Anthony sound asleep, his cheek on the bar.

"Well, I guess that answers my question."

CHAPTER 23

In the dark twilight hours, the ramshackle city of Caltesia was only slightly less busy. As they approached the edge of town, Alex saw less and less of the people outside the opening in their buggy/cart. She wasn't sure what to call it at this point. Alex thought back to their time in town, and she was sad to be leaving. Despite their encounter with the magical assassins, this city had provided the only true reprieve from the weight of the daunting task that lay before them. It was the first time in their mission that she felt like she had finally achieved their initial objective to explore. What's more, it felt like her old days in the military, getting to travel far and wide and see new cultures and people up close. Now though, their group was well outside of town.

"This is the spot," Fraygor called from behind Alex.

"You sure?"

Fraygor responded with a pointed finger and Alex followed it to a dim glowing green lantern hanging from a tree. Another tree was parallel, and between them a large rock. Everyone got out, but drivers Isaac and Darius.

"So, where is the entrance?" Alex wondered aloud.

Hef'krost had been cryptic about their destination, mostly giving them directions out of town and telling them to look for a green lantern.

"It will be hidden, the dwarves are a guarded people when it comes to outsiders," said Fraygor.

"Well, if I had a secret country underneath another country I'd be pretty secretive too." said Alex.

According to Hef'krost, there was a dwarven nation hidden in the cave network beneath Kestalia. Hidden was generous, dwarves were a known race in this world, but they kept to themselves, or so Fraygor had said. The entrances to the underground were well kept secrets, their only ways to the surface.

"The entrance will likely be some sort of hidden mechanism, perhaps one protected by some sort of puzzle. Dwarves do like their riddles." Fraygor mused, "But we shouldn't expect it to be easy to…"

Loud rumbling and the rock ahead of them tilted upwards, suddenly alight with glowing green runes.

Charlie pulled on the lantern. She looked back at the group.

Fraygor looked stunned.

"Oh, come on, it was obvious! Let's go!" she shouted, and hopped off the hill of dirt the tree grew out of.

Alex laughed at Fraygor's confused expression when Charlie ran back to the vehicles.

"Charlie, before we head down there, I need you to get out the drone."

Charlie's eyes widened, "I've been waiting literally days for you to say that." she bolted to the back of the rear buggy, excitement evident on her face.

Soon, the robot buzzed high above them, the whine of its motors now barely audible.

"Datalink is set up, boss, the drone is talking to the radio balloon," said Charlie.

Alex held the radio up to her face. "Pyetro? Are you there?" There was a brief silence, and a crackle, followed by a familiar voice.

"Alex! We've been worried about you guys," Pyetro said over the slight static of the radio.

"Yeah, sorry about the radio silence, we've been busy. How are things there?"

"Kairnos took some folks to the village, and they welcomed us with open arms. Some of them have even started visiting the outpost."

"That's good Pyetro, just wanted to check on you guys a bit, we're gonna be underground for a while." She realized how strange that last sentence sounded.

"Oh, you away team people, always getting all the adventures. Good luck to you and your team. Talk to us when you can, we'll 'hold down the fort' as you Americans say," Pyetro ended with a chuckle.

"We will. Talk to you soon. Alex out," she turned the radio off. "Sounds like they're okay, let's get the drone down and head out—or I guess head *down.*"

Charlie brought down the drone, and everyone loaded back up.

They cautiously drove the vehicles down into the hole under the rock. It was a tight fit as they drove slowly over a sharp decline at the entrance, then down a gentle slope, slick with moisture. They trudged along carefully.

Dirt and mud transitioned gradually into a more solid rocky surface. The tunnel was relatively narrow, and the walls were lined with glowing runic symbols.

Alex studied them closely; they almost looked like hieroglyphics, although she wasn't exactly an expert on the matter. As she passed by them, they gradually curved farther away as the tunnel got wider. Eventually, the walls weren't visible anymore, replaced by eerie pitch blackness.

They continued to move downward when Fraygor said, "Your people have a great many fascinating devices, Alex."

"Yes, we do. I'm guessing you guys don't have ways of talking over long distances?"

"There are some magics, but nothing as simple or quick as your machines. I must admit I'm jealous of that ability."

Alex looked over her shoulder, "Got someone you want to talk to? Special someone?" she finished with a smirk.

Fraygor cracked a grin, "I won't bore you with the details."

"That's a yes," Darius chuckled, joining in on the conversation, still focused on the road.

Alex rolled her eyes jokingly and looked ahead.

The dark was oppressive, the headlights doing their best to show the way, but failing past a certain distance. Alex had expected it to be rockier and windier, but this was a flat and *very* straight path.

"So, tell me about these dwarves, Fraygor," said Alex.

"Hardy people, although they don't like magic, almost despise it." he said.

"Really?" Darius asked. "If I had magic I wouldn't want to give it up."

"Darius, I would say that your 'technology' as you call it is more advanced than many magics," Fraygor used the English word amongst the ones being translated.

"Fair enough."

"The dwarves rely on complex machinations, mostly powered by a magnetic ore they call Zhondier," Fraygor continued.

"Oh gosh, don't tell Charlie that, she'll want to steal some," Alex joked. "Will we be seeing some dwarves soon?"

Fraygor peered out the window, "It is hard to say, the underground is a vast landscape beneath that of the surface. We may travel the whole way without encountering a single settlement."

The slope ended, and they were now across more open ground, no longer in a tunnel. A faint path lay ahead, but the darkness remained ever present. Hef'krost hadn't given them a map per say, but rather a series of directions that boiled down to which turns to make and when.

"At least we don't have to worry about assassins anymore. They can't possibly find us down here," said Darius.

"True, but Mister Darius there may well be other dangers. I myself am not well-versed in the underground, but I have heard of rather strange creatures. I do hope that your 'cannon' is effective on them."

Alex thought back to the rear buggy, with Calseous, Alicia, Charlie, and Isaac. Anthony was asleep in Alex's buggy across from Fraygor. It took a lot to convince Fraygor to separate from Calseous, but Alex wanted the capable fighters to spread out, and she wanted the prince in the vehicle with the big gun.

"Charlie," Alex said over her radio. "What sort of optics do we have on that cannon?"

Charlie's voice came through the other end very warbly and unclear for a moment, but eventually became clearer. *"J—t the — an—rd —uff boss. Low light optics, but those aren't any use in pitch blackness like this. I have thermal imaging but that's only really showing me faint outlines in the dark. I can't really see where we're going, but it should be helpful if anyone or anything sneaks up on us though. This is awesome, I might finally get to shoot something with this thing."*

Alex chuckled, "Copy that, Charlie, keep your eyes peeled. How long do you suppose it'll take us to get there, Fraygor?"

He stroked the stubble of his beard. "It is hard to say, I'm not familiar with your machines. Were I to guess, I would say it could not take more than two days' journey. Much faster than our original plan since we are now traveling *under* the mountain range rather than around it."

"That's still a while," said Darius.

Alex nodded and looked forward once again.

After a few minutes of silence, Darius spoke up, "So, Fraygor, I think we have enough free time to hear the boring details about your romantic interest," he said in an altogether mischievous tone.

Alex chuckled, "I suppose we do," she added, keeping her eyes locked ahead of her.

The old guard captain sighed wearily. "I am afraid it is not entirely my story to tell. It would not be fair to my dear lady for me to divulge."

Alex and Darius shared a sideways glance.

"That's a very eloquent, *'it's complicated'* my friend!" said Darius. He seemed more intrigued now than before.

Darius had done this a couple of times at home base on their brief break after the Orc battle. He seemed to know the exact line between making someone uncomfortable and getting them to be honest. Alex had experienced this first-hand.

Fraygor chuckled. "I'm afraid that does not come close to covering it. We would need far more time, a secluded location, and many drinks for me to explain it in entirety."

This was the most casual Fraygor had ever been with them. Alex was almost afraid to speak and risk the stoic man changing his mind.

Darius however, had no qualms, "You do realize that makes me more intrigued right? I am more than willing to meet those requirements once we're in the capital." Darius briefly looked away from the road and back at Fraygor. "I'll even pay for the drinks, somehow-"

Alex was looking ahead of the group and saw a glint of light. The glint shifted into the silhouette of a shiny insect-like creature.

It instantly lunged directly at them.

"Darius!" Alex screamed.

He spun around and jerked the wheel to the left.

The creature was now headed directly to the side of the transport, right next to Alex's seat.

The buggy jostled side to side as the beast's added weight displaced the center of balance. Alex struggled to retrieve her sidearm.

Only faint rays of reflected light outlined its form, but Alex could make out a long thin *beak* attempting to peek its way through the narrow open windows. With each repeating thud it failed to breach the gaps between the ramshackle wooden planks covering their otherwise modern vehicle.

It finally found a hole and a spindly spider-like leg entered the cabin through the window. Alex pressed herself against Darius to give herself more distance and kicked the appendage. It collapsed with a sickening crack, followed by a shrill screech.

Alex pulled out an emergency flare, the first thing she could grab.

"Darius, stop!" She commanded and twisted the top of the flare. It snapped open and she tossed it, the flash nearly blinding her.

The beast's cries intensified as it detached from them, and the transport snapped back to the left.

"Charlie, low light NOW!" She tried to sound calm over the radio, but knew she failed.

Unintelligible static crackled over the radio, but she felt sure it was coming from Charlie.

Four loud and closely linked snaps sounded in the darkness; each briefly illuminated their surroundings. Now they had four less cannon rounds. In the brief cannon's flashes, Alex was shocked they couldn't see the ceiling, or any walls of the cave. They were out in the open, and from the window, and under the red glow of the flare, she could see a slumped over tangle of spindly limbs, and a black shiny center.

"Do you see that Darius?"

He nodded but said nothing.

Suddenly a similar shriek, far more distant.

"Get back on the road, Darius."

Alex got back on the radio. "Charlie?"

Charlie shouted, "Drive boss!"

Alex didn't even need the radio to hear her.

"How many?"

"Just *drive!*"

Darius pushed hard on the pedal slamming everyone back in their seats.

Anthony yelled, "Alex!"

She turned and he handed her another flare. Alex cracked open the new flare and held it outside the window. She could see a dozen more of those black shells. Suddenly, startled by a chorus of shrieks from the mass of creatures, Alex nearly dropped the flare.

She turned anxiously toward Darius.

"Alex, I'm going as fast as I can! I can't see very well!"

The creatures were nearly keeping up with them, staying right alongside their transport.

Alex heard more cannonfire, but it wasn't aimed at the creatures she could see in front of her. They indeed looked like some sort of insect, or spider or maybe even a crab, but they had a beak, almost like that of a squid, albeit longer and thinner.

The beak protruded from a helmet-like shell that raised and lowered with their shrieks. They ran on four stronger legs, with two thinner but clawed appendages on either side of their beak. As she got a good look at them, something peculiar became apparent. While the glint from their shell was constant in the light, the other parts of its body faded in and out of view, intermittently obstructed by a smoky black gaseous substance that poured from under the shell. Following a brief interruption of the shooting, the horde before her was dashed away by Charlie's 'big gun'. The shrieks grew quieter on the right side, and louder on the other. Alex saw there were now dozens of the shadowy black creatures now sprinting alongside Darius.

Alex called through her radio, "Charlie how are we on ammo?"

"Twenty shots left, boss, then I gotta reload us. Do we have a plan?"

"Fire sparingly, only hit the ones that are getting close. I'll think of something."

Alex looked back to Fraygor, "Any clue what these things are?"

"I am as baffled as you I'm afraid. Whatever they are, they're ravenous."

"Why didn't Hef'krost tell us about these things?" Alex took the chance to finally grab her sidearm from its holster.

One of the spindly legs broke through the ceiling of the vehicle, and slashed through Darius' coat, directly into his shoulder.

Darius cried out, "Gah!" but he kept driving. The leg retreated, but a screaming beak poked through immediately.

Alex raised her weapon and squeezed the trigger, aiming squarely between the creature's jaws. Perfect hit, and the beast was sent flying. Despite the noise-suppression the weapons usually offered, in this enclosed space the shot had left her ears ringing.

"Darius?!"

Alex inspected the gash, when smoke started seeping from the wound; the same smoke coming from the creatures.

It was obvious Darius was in pain. His shoulder went limp, and his entire body slumped forward.

Alex jumped back, her heart nearly stopped, but her instincts took over. "Anthony, tell the others to stop!"

She pressed down on Darius' knee hoping to engage the vehicle's brakes. The wheels screeched as they skidded along the slick stone surface, but they finally jolted to a stop.

She yanked the parking brake. "Anthony, do we have more flares?"

He handed her one more emergency flare before drawing his weapon.

The other vehicle skidded behind them. Alex jumped out and was nearly blinded by its headlights. She shielded her eyes from the beams and cracked open her last flare, relieved to see none of the creatures immediately around them.

As the other transports stopped, the roaring din of scrambling legs and shrieking beaks came from behind. Alex turned and tossed the flare as far as she could. It landed with a thud on the head of the beast at the front of the swarm, immediately rearing and then falling on its back. The other creatures avoided the flare, kept their distance as they deftly swarmed past.

Isaac leaped out of the rear transport and tossed two lit flares.

He yelled, "Boss, they hate the light!"

"Anthony!"

"On it!"

Alex quickly checked Darius' pulse, it was weak, but steady. More cannons cracked. Breathing a sigh of relief, she jumped out with Anthony and Fraygor.

Charlie climbed out of the other buggy. "Outta cannon!"

The stout woman took two flares, bit the caps off with her teeth and laid them out on each side of their transport. "Make a circle of flares, that should keep 'em away!"

Anthony followed Charlie's example and laid out flares uniformly. With the dropped flares and headlights, they now had a circle of light between them and the monsters.

With no way of crossing the light barrier without exposing themselves, the creatures swarmed around them in a massive swirling cyclone. They marched continuously around the perimeter.

A concerned Isaac said, "Boss these flares last thirty minutes tops, we have to figure something out."

Alex looked around them, it was hard to gauge exact numbers, but she knew just by glancing they didn't have enough ammo for their sidearms to take out all of these creature's even if they hit every shot perfectly.

"Charlie, how many cannon rounds are left in the spare canisters?"

"Not enough, that's for sure. You can't see all of these things without the thermal camera but there are literally hundreds of 'em!"

Alex studied the encroaching monsters. "Okay, let's all calm down. We're safe for now, but we need a plan."

Suddenly, the creatures halted, jolting to a stop in unison, and turned in the same direction, but Alex couldn't see why.

The cave was quiet now; their crawling had ceased, leaving only the hissing of the lit flares, and occasional shrieks from the beasts.

In the silence, Alex heard a sensation; a vibration in her ears, but she couldn't feel anything. As it pounded in her head, she noticed the transport's suspension wobbling. They swayed rhythmically with the vibrations Alex could now feel in her feet.

"What is *that?"*

"What is what?" Anthony looked confused.

"Listen."

The group hushed. The sensation grew heavier in her ears. It wasn't just a rhythm, it was…a *beat.*

The silence slowly waned as the swarm began to emit a low hissing noise, but was quickly overwhelmed by the sound of drums.

"Music?" said Alex.

"What the…"

Charlie was interrupted by the bellowing of a distant, deep horn.

Some of the swarm fled away, but others crawled towards the music. In the distance was a bright green glow, the same shade as on the runic symbols. The glow was framed by a curious silhouette.

Three high-pitched pops and a salvo of bright blue shimmering lights shot from the mystery object. The entire area lit up, and the insect's fled in droves.

The music got louder, mainly the sounds of drums and horns. A heavy and irreverent tempo reminded Alex of twentieth century rock from back on Earth.

In the newfound light, their apparent saviors stood on top of a large metal vehicle; about twenty short, stocky people, most with beards.

"Dwarves," said Fraygor casually.

"No way!" Charlie seemed to marvel at the machinery rather than the alien race before them.

One dwarf in a snug fitting helmet, hopped down and approached Alex. He looked her up and down, took off his helmet, craned his neck, and stared her in the eyes.

There was only silence, other than the beating drums.

Alex had no clue what to say to a dwarf, and the rest of the team seemed too shocked to speak. The dwarf in front of Alex scowled. "Ka'rak Moraz. Bek corr'laan."

Oh yay, this again.

Alex sighed, "Alicia!"

CHAPTER 24

DESPITE HER BEST EFFORTS, Alicia couldn't get anything substantial translated. Even speaking the language of the Castalia kingdom didn't change things.

Finally, the dwarf grumbled something and walked away.

"I'm not sure what to do Alex, I have no reference whatsoever for their language and it's different from Kastalian." Alicia admitted.

Alex tried to concentrate but with the continuous pounding of the drums and horns it was difficult to form any coherent thoughts.

The dwarven transport rolled towards them, and slowly creaked to a stop.

Now Alex could see that the top of the vehicle had a sort of platform. Six of them pounded away on drums almost as big as they were.

The platform had large horns at the front and rear, similar to Swiss Matterhorn's on Earth but curved in many places like a rudimentary tuba.

Alex was curious, and frustrated, with the persistent sound of the instruments. Why did the dwarves play them—constantly?

Dressed a little more modestly, a second dwarf approached them with no armor of any kind, and a thick braided ginger beard.

"I'm told you speak the human language from above?" he said with a deep and gravelly voice.

Alex and Alicia shared a surprised glance.

"Yes?" Alex asked.

The short man smirked. "Are you unsure of this?"

"No, we just weren't expecting you to speak it." said Alicia.

"I am one of the few that do, and so they bring me on these patrols."

Puzzled, Alex asked, "Patrols?"

He shrugged. "Patrols to keep swarms of the shadow scarred away."

Alex thought of Darius' wound and the black gas the creatures spewed.

"You mean those bug creatures. My friend was sliced by one of them."

The dwarf's eyes widened, "Then we have no time to lose. Quickly, follow us." He ran back to his vehicle and climbed aboard.

"That was abrupt." Alicia followed Alex back to the buggies.

Isaac helped Alex move Darius into the back of the vehicle. She took the driver's seat and looked back at her wounded friend. "Hang on, Darius." But she wasn't sure if he could hear her.

Alex started to follow the dwarves, but their strange transport suddenly darted forward, instantly bolting away from them. Alex stomped on the gas and tried to keep up.

They followed for about an hour when the dwarves started weaving through a narrower section of the underground, a winding path that took them around stalactites and boulders.

The dwarves navigated the tricky paths with confidence. Alex struggled to keep up but they weren't cutting her any slack. It wasn't long before the area above the path became more illuminated by that same green light.

Just after passing by a particularly large pillar, they were met with a massive door, cut into the walls of the cave, that blocked the way forward. Cleanly constructed from stone and metal, with simple adornments, it was dotted with the same glowing runes.

All vehicles halted in front of the structure. The music abruptly stopped, but the sudden brief silence was almost immediately pierced by the loudest horn Alex had ever heard. It was coming from the dwarven transport.

The horn gradually lowered and the largest rune above the door began blinking. It blinked rapidly then went dark. The horn slowly ceased.

The door slowly opened from the center, the two sections disappearing into the frame.

The dwarven vehicle slowly moved forward.

Alex cautiously followed.

Once past the door, the naturally formed roughness of the narrow tunnel they had traveled through was gone, replaced with one neatly cut out of the rock.

Shortly they passed through an opening into a *much* larger room. The dwarves pulled their vehicle up against a ledge that ran the length of the room; perfectly elevated to allow them to step off.

Some sort of loading dock? Alex wasn't sure, but she saw a set of stairs near where the ledge ended and opted to park there.

Darius was now sweating and flushed. Exiting their transports, Alex and Isaac hoisted him up once again. The clattering of heavy boots accompanied several dwarves including their friend from earlier.

"This is your friend who was hurt, correct?" he asked Alex.

"Yeah, there's some sort of weird smoke coming out of his cut."

"Then it's good you brought him here." he turned to the other dwarves. "Ko'tzak! Fe'roh moro moro moro!"

Quickly, two came and gestured for Alex to let them take Darius.

One said firmly, "Za'twoke."

Alex was hesitant, but she didn't have any better options. She watched as the short men struggled to carry—drag really, the hefty

Darius. They seemed strong enough, but they struggled, and Darius' legs scraped against the floor.

So far, the dwarves varied slightly in height, but none of them were as short as Alex had expected. The one she could talk with appeared to be roughly four and half feet tall.

Alex was still concerned. "Where are they taking him?"

"To the healers; they will do their best."

Alex watched the two dwarfs load Darius onto some sort of stretcher.

She raised her brow, "Their best?"

"The shadow scarred attacks affect everyone differently, to say nothing of their effects on surface folk."

Alex raised her voice, "Haven't you treated humans before?"

"Not in quite some time. In the rare case that humans do enter the underground, they seldom visit us. If any of them happen to come upon a swarm of shadow scarred, they are most often gone by the time we reach them."

Alex watched as the medical dwarves carried Darius away but heard steps approaching and turned to see her team.

Isaac looked past Alex to Darius, "Where are they taking him, boss?"

"To get help, that's all I really know."

"Well, is he going to be okay?" asked Charlie.

"They aren't sure," Alex wasn't sure how else to put it.

Anthony walked past the group, but Alex grabbed his shoulder.

Anthony stopped and faced her, "I should be there, healing you guys is my responsibility."

"Anthony, we have no idea what this stuff is."

Anthony jerked away from her.

Alex took a deep breath, "Anthony, medifoam might make it *worse*. I hate to say it but, we should leave it to the experts."

Anthony sighed but didn't say anything. He walked back to Alicia's side.

Fraygor stepped forward and addressed their dwarven friend. "Greetings, I am Fraygor, head guard of Prince Calseous of Kestalia," he raised a hand in a gesture towards the prince.

Alex noticed that Calseous seemed shaken by their encounter.

The ginger bearded dwarf nodded at Fraygor. "Well met, I am Erdueril."

"We are attempting to get to the capital of the kingdom, this detour, and Darius' wounds complicate things. May I ask that you provide us a secure location to keep the prince safe?" said Fraygor.

"Within these walls you are safe, no assassins will find their way here."

Fraygor squinted, "I take it you are Hef'krost's contact?"

Erdueril smiled a wide toothy smile, "Indeed, he told me you would be coming.

"I am grateful you arrived when you did."

Alex approached the pair, "How did you scare off those bug things?"

"The Ku'qerw of my people!" he said proudly, pointing at the large drums on their transport. "The beasts are greatly affected by noise. They are attracted to higher pitches but lower and deeper sounds damage their innards."

So that's why they played them the entire time they were in the caves.

"They don't seem to like light either," said Alex.

"Indeed, our runes keep our towns safe from the swarms," said Erdueril. "I must say I am impressed you lasted as long as you did." He walked towards the buggies. "Your vehicles seem to be falling apart."

The exterior wooden makeover they had given them had been smashed to pieces, with many planks completely gone.

Charlie grabbed a loosely hanging plank from a buggy and pulled it off. "So much for blending in," she said. "Boss, we should remove the rest of these. It's not really safe to have splintered wood and nails falling on us the whole trip."

Charlie nodded to Isaac, and he started helping her remove the wooden scraps.

As more and more of the original frame of the buggy was revealed, Erdueril's eyes widened.

"Gods below, you are not normal surface folk are you? I had not seen that your carriages had no animals carrying them."

"They're electric." Charlie pulled more planks and hefted them to the ground.

Erdueril looked confused. "Electric?"

Alex realized that this word wasn't translating to Kestalian.

"I guess you could say powered by...invisible energy." Charlie said.

"Without zhondier?"

"'Zon'? What now?"

Erdueril walked around one of their transports, inspecting it in great detail.

"I have the feeling that our artificers will wish to speak with you, miss—what was your name?"

"Charlie."

Isaac climbed on the top of the vehicle and tore the coverings off the cannon.

Erdueril asked, "Some sort of weapon?"

"Yes, it's a Mk-207 light autocannon. Pretty small but the ammo and optics are really high quality," said Charlie.

"That cannon is the only reason we made it," Alex pointed out.

Alex looked over to Anthony and Alicia, both of whom looked tired and weary.

She asked, "Erdueril, is there any place for my people to rest? We've come a long way on very little sleep."

"Of course. Kro'zhak!" he shouted something, and a young dwarf approached, his small beard much less impressive than Erdueril's.

Erdueril pointed at Alicia and Anthony and spoke a long sentence in his language; Alex couldn't even begin to follow.

The younger dwarf led Anthony and Alicia hopefully to get some sleep.

With half of her team now going to rest, and the other half preoccupied with the vehicles, Alex turned her attention to Fraygor and the prince.

"How are you two holding up?" she asked both of them, but with her eyes locked on the prince. He was looking around, and it seemed to Alex he was more afraid than curious.

"We're unharmed, but we must move as quickly as we can," said Fraygor "Calseous was expected back two days ago. There have been enough detours, any longer and his enemies in the court will only seize on this opportunity to discredit him."

"As soon as Darius is well, we'll move," said Alex.

Fraygor grumbled as he and the prince walked away.

Alex understood his impatience, but she had to worry about her people first. She could only hope at this point that her decision to come here would make the difference in saving Darius.

CHAPTER 25

Alex woke up but with no natural light, she had no idea what time it was or how long she had slept. She stood, stretched, and checked her wrist-computer. The best estimate was based on the last time they had seen the sun, she had been out for eleven hours. She felt guilty sleeping that long, but they were all exhausted. She was sure everyone had rested better in a proper bed.

Dwarven beds were remarkably comfortable, definitely better than anything else she had seen in this world. They had graciously given each of her team their own room with a bed, and a bathroom with actual plumbing. It seemed the dwarves were more advanced than the surface world, or at least more in-line with Earth's development. Alex was more comfortable in this environment than Caltesia, as fascinating as the port city had been, it was also incredibly hectic.

The spartan and simple interior of the dwarven settlement reminded her of her time in the military, similar to some of the navy ships she had visited, but less cramped. On top of all that, Alex would take running water over magic *any* day.

She left her room, and entered the main concourse of the settlement, an impossibly long hallway. Erdueril had explained a bit about the settlement earlier. He showed Alex a map showing the settlement's layout, and she was surprised to learn this was one of the smaller towns. Built on a grid with four rows and four columns, each had an adjacent carved, massive corridor.

Between the corridors were buildings carved into the stone. It was like a gargantuan fallout shelter, mixed with an underground shopping mall. It appeared they had everything they needed down here, they even grew crops with artificial lights.

Alex headed towards the medical ward to check on Darius. She wasn't sure where everyone else was; she had slept longer than any of them, but Darius was her first stop regardless.

She passed several dwarfs who all gawked at her.

Being a more than average tall human woman in dwarf-land was a step above simply standing out. Still, everyone was friendly; gruff, but friendly.

Erdueril had told her how to find the medical ward, identified by a hanging sign with a medical symbol. The room was small, and through a window on the opposite wall she could see several dwarfs surrounding Darius in what looked like an operating room.

She pushed the door open and heard Anthony's voice.

"Alex."

She turned to see Anthony and Isaac sitting in some seats carved out of the stone.

Anthony said, "They're doing some sort of operation. I couldn't tell much; I haven't been able to speak with them."

Alex thought he looked glum, and she turned back where Darius lay.

The dwarfs were wearing curious outfits, similar to the simple armor pieces they wore the day before. The gaps between the armor sections were filled with some sort of animal hide or leather material.

At least it will keep the beard hairs out of his wounds.

She sat next to Isaac, sighed, and clasped her hands.

"He's been in there for two hours, boss," said Isaac." It's scary not even knowing how he's doing. We're totally in the dark."

Alex looked at the two men, "Where's Alicia?"

"She's working with that Kestalian speaking dwarf to try and update our translators with the dwarven language," said Anthony.

Alex looked at the floor. From the corner of her eye, she noticed Isaac and Anthony's heads hung as low as hers.

"I guess the hospital waiting room experience is universal," she said half-heartedly.

There was no response, probably not the best time for humor. A vibration from her wrist computer grabbed her attention.

'Language database updated'.

Alex stood immediately, "That was fast, Alicia got us translations."

She ticked the box 'Dwarvish' on her device, and the voices throughout the clinic shifted from the alien language to English. Alicia really was something else.

One of the female Dwarven doctors exited the operating room.

Alex crossed the room to her. "How is he doing?"

The dwarf, obviously surprised by Alex's sudden fluency in her language, removed her headgear, "Still too early to tell, we've never seen a reaction like this to an infection.

Anthony joined Alex, "React how?"

"His body is rejecting the shadow infection, which is good. We are trying to extract the shadow itself, but there is a lot of damage to his tissue."

Anthony furrowed his brow, "This 'shadow', do you mean the black gas from the monsters?"

"Yes. The shadow is a creature of its own, the shadow scarred simply acts as its hosts and infectors. It is trying to attach itself to his blood, but since it's being rejected, it seems to be killing him."

"What's preventing the extraction?" asked Anthony.

"The creature moves around in his body quicker than we can find it. We've never seen something like this before, even after pouring over ancient records." she replied.

Alex barely followed the medical discussion, but it still caused her to worry more.

Anthony said, "Alex, I think I can help them. I have some imaging equipment that might detect where the infection is and when it moves."

"Anthony, whatever you can do, do it."

Alex nodded.

The doctor said, "You have some advanced machinations? If you can provide us any help I would gladly accept it. We don't have much time."

Anthony followed the dwarven doctor, putting Alex a little at ease. With the Dwarves' knowledge and Anthony's equipment, this might be the best chance Darius had.

Alex placed her hand on the glass and watched her friend through the window. Darius lay on a raised platform, seemingly made of marble. His skin was discolored, especially around his lips, and he was sweating. The wound in his shoulder was much larger than the small gash he had originally suffered, like he had picked at it for several months and never let it heal. It hadn't even been a day, if it kept up at this rate…

Alex shook her head and looked away. Isaac had his head in his hands. She left the window and took a seat next to him.

"Isaac? Are you alright?"

Tears leaked from the corners of Isaac's eyes. "I just wish I could talk to him; you know? The last real conversation we had together was all trash talk. I feel like such a jerk, and if that's the last thing I ever said to him…"

Alex could feel his pain, and without thinking she said the first thing that came to her mind, "If it's the last thing you ever did with him, then he'll remember you as his friend."

Isaac inhaled and then let the air escape his lungs. "You think so?"

Alex usually avoided difficult conversations, but something in her was pushing her to keep talking to Isaac.

"Isaac, I don't think Darius would want to spend his last day any other way than dumb fun with his friends."

Isaac's eyes were red, "You're right, boss."

Alex reluctantly placed a hand on his shoulder, "Anthony says he has a plan to help Darius. I don't know why, but I think it's going to be okay."

Isaac nodded, even cracking a slight smile as he looked past her towards the operating room, "Okay. Thanks, boss."

Alex stood. "I better go see what everyone else is up to. You stay here and keep an eye on Darius, okay?"

Isaac nodded, still staring at the operating room window.

Alex had no clue where Charlie and Alicia were, so she wandered around the settlement. She decided to head back to the entrance to see if anyone was with the buggies.

She was not expecting to see Charlie, hands on her hips, a crowd of dwarves around her. She was perched atop the armed vehicle addressing the crowd.

"And this vehicle's battery can be recharged by the power of the sun." she shouted. Alex walked down the stairs. She watched Charlie pull out what she called her *baby,* the big custom rifle she had used to snipe the orcs. She unfolded the weapon, then rattled off a list of the gun's specs at the same time she grabbed something from her pack.

Charlie tossed a paper plate like a frisbee, quickly following it with her weapon. She placed a shot straight through it, splitting it in half. A bellowing cheer erupted from the gathered dwarves, and Charlie beamed and soaked in their admiration.

"My own design too," she said.

"Charlie!" Alex waved at the red-haired woman.

Alex might have gone unnoticed in the crowd were she not nearly two feet taller than them.

Charlie hopped down off the transport. "These guys are amazing! They're the artificers or whatever, the engineers and inventors of the dwarves. It's crazy, they don't understand a word I'm sayin', but they're hangin' on every last one."

"You do know that Alicia updated our translators with their language, right?"

Charlie's eyes widened and she looked down at her own wrist computer, deftly navigating to the translator page and applying the update.

"Hey guys!" She shouted to the crowd, "I can speak Dwarf now!"

Another cheer erupted from the dwarves. Charlie was approached by half a dozen of them with question after question.

Alex chuckled and walked away; Charlie was going to be busy. She was laughing more than she had since they first met.

"Ha Ha! I have found my people!" she yelled.

Alex shook her head and continued up the stairs. She was glad Charlie was happy, she just hoped she wouldn't have to drag her kicking and screaming when it was time to leave.

CHAPTER 26

NOW THAT SHE COULD SPEAK Dwarvish, it wasn't that hard to find help locating Alicia. Alex wondered if there was a single resident of the town that wasn't aware of their presence. Word seemed to travel fast in this insular community. Following directions from a passerby, she nearly bumped into Alicia when they both rounded a corner.

"Alex!" Alicia blurted. "Sorry. I'm not operating on a ton of sleep right now."

"No problem. I can't believe you already got us translations Alicia, I'm not sure you understand how amazing that is."

"Thanks," Alicia groaned, clearly not paying attention.

"Where are you headed?"

"To see Darius, I'm worried about him."

"C'mon, I'll take you there."

Alex walked with her towards the medical ward and watched Alicia wobble with each step; her eyes were barely open.

"Actually, I don't think that's the best idea right now, Alicia. You need sleep. How long have you been awake?"

"Two hours, or wait, did I *sleep* for two hours? I'm not entirely sure." She stopped a moment and pondered the question.

"Okay, I'm taking you back to your room. You're going to pass out before you even get to the doctor." Alex put her hands on

Alicia's shoulders and stopped her.

Alicia mumbled something, only Darius' name was clear.

"Come on, you've earned a warm dwarf bed."

"Boss!" Isaac was running towards her.

Out of breath he said, "Darius is going into surgery with Anthony and the Dwarf doctors."

Alicia mumbled, "Surgery?"

Alex wasn't sure if that was a good or bad thing, but she knew she needed to know more.

"Isaac, take Alicia to get some rest and then meet me at the clinic."

"You got it boss." Isaac put his arm around Alicia's shoulder and led her away.

Alex ran as fast as she could, probably scaring more than a few of the residents when she sprinted through the hallways. Through the medical ward's window, she could see Anthony and a half-dozen dwarven doctors standing over Darius' unconscious body.

Anthony held an imaging device a few inches above his friend's chest. It was one of the portable models they gave field medics. Alex thought they looked a bit like a plastic dry iron. With Anthony's free hand he held a tablet that was connected to the device in his other hand via a cable. The doctors were clearly fascinated.

Alex couldn't hear what they were saying, but she could see Anthony's mouth moving underneath the surgical mask he was wearing. As he lingered over Darius' left leg, he spoke louder. Two of the short doctors moved into action, one lifting Darius' leg up and the other quickly and precisely beginning to cut…

Alex closed her eyes. She wasn't great with needles, let alone scalpels. Her eyes remained shut until she heard a boisterous cheer from the operating room.

She peeked an eye open to see one of the Dwarven surgeons holding a bizarre object between a pair of tweezers. It was both spiky, gooey, and had a purplish-black tint to it. It was glinting in the bright overhead lighting of the surgery suite.

Wisps of smoky black gas trailed from it when a dwarf moved it across the room. He carefully placed it into a stone container.

With the lid closed and sealed, Alex could once again hear some verbal adulation directed towards Anthony. Alex would have expected a round of handshakes, instead it seemed the Dwarven equivalent was a firm bear-hug, most of which Anthony seemed to be enduring with a nervous smile.

The color had started to return to Darius' face, and relief washed over Alex. Once Anthony could get free, he applied medifoam to Darius' injury and incision. Probably best to do it while Darius was still unconscious, that way it wouldn't hurt.

Alex could see Isaac in the reflection of the glass.

He was out of breath when he reached her, "Any news?"

"I'm no expert, but it looks like it went well. At the very least they got that thing out of him."

Isaac's face relaxed, "Really? Just like that?"

Alex smiled, "Miracles of modern medicine, even in another world. Did you get Alicia to rest?"

"She was asleep way before she got to her bed. She's out, like a rock."

"Good."

Alex sighed, walked away from the window, and took a seat. With the looming specter of a direly injured team-member out of the way, it was time to start thinking about next steps.

It took a few hours, and a *lot* of walking around, but Alex gathered everyone together. She wouldn't have thought they were ready to travel, but Fraygor insisted time was running out, and Erdueril had promised them an escort.

Charlie tearfully hugged no less than twenty dwarves, promising them that she would be back one day.

Darius was still unconscious and Alicia barely awake, but they loaded them in the rear of the armed buggy, and the team set out. Driving the buggy, Alex trailed behind the much larger dwarven transport. She followed closer this time.

From the passenger seat Erdueril said, "Your vehicles handle the rough terrain rather well, I'm a bit jealous. Ours ride rough."

"Your—what do you call that thing?" Alex asked.

"A war wagon, and yes it is very bumpy."

Alex found it easier to talk to Erdueril, all of the dwarves really, since they spoke more casually. Most of the other folks in this world spoke in what Alex thought of as 'olde timey' speech.

Calseous for example, spoke formally, fancily, and it kind of annoyed Alex. The dwarves however, casually got to the point right away.

"Why do you call it a war wagon?"

"We refer to our fight against the shadow scarred as a war."

Alex asked, "Aren't they just monsters? Animals basically?"

"No, they aren't just beasts, they're a plague, and one that we must deal with. It is our duty."

"Duty?"

"The shadow scarred are not natural beasts, they are…our great shame. A thousand years ago, the Dwarven clans lived and traded with the surface freely, but not without conflict. After one too many fights with the humans and elves, a plot was hatched to retreat underground and ensure that no-one would ever bother us again."

Alex raised an eyebrow.

"The shadow scarred are the result of that plan, an ancient curse unleashed on the underground to act as a barrier between us and the surface. The madmen who did this did not speak for the rest of the clans, but few did anything to stop them. The pain of the conflicts they experienced left them numb, that's my guess at least." Erdueril continued.

"You're telling me that those things were *made* by the dwarves?" Alex asked.

"Not made really." Erdueril sounded frustrated. "The shadow scarred are what happens when someone is left to succumb to the infection of the curse. The mages who unleashed this neglected to mention the more gruesome aspects of their plan." His disdain was obvious, but he continued.

"By the time the clans realized what was happening, it was too late. Each victim the beasts take only bolsters their numbers. When an elven army ventured into the underground, they weren't prepared for what awaited them, and the shadow scarred became a massive force overnight."

Alex couldn't believe what she was hearing, "So, the shadow scarred—they're people that are—transformed?"

"I'm afraid so. As I said, this is our great shame."

Alex didn't even want to think about what would have happened if Darius hadn't been seen by dwarven doctors, especially given this new information.

"So, you're planning on taking them all out?"

"Every last one, no matter how long it takes. A war of many generations, yes, but one that is ours to wage."

Alex couldn't help but resonate with the sense of duty he had. She had always wanted to join the military, like her parents, but duty was what finally got her to enlist. Seeing the news coming out of the pacific war, the cruelty of the enemies and the suffering of so many people, she felt compelled. What a concept, *duty*, an obligation born of one's morality.

"When I get home…*if* I get home, I'll talk to some folks about seeing how we can help."

Erdueril's eyes widened, "Your people would help? Your 'United Nations'?"

That caught Alex off guard. "How did you hear about them?"

"Your friend, Alicia. She told me much about your world, and in exchange I taught her much about us. Our language, our culture. It was very pleasant." Erdueril said, a smile on his bearded face.

Alex's instinct was to worry about the mission, but once again it occurred to her that the original objective wasn't in play anymore. Get home, get her people home, no matter what. That was the mission now. No more secrecy, not when it wasn't necessary at least.

"I can't promise anything, but yeah, I'll see if we can help. You think this little cannon is powerful, just wait," Alex smirked.

"Don't tempt me Alex. Your Charlie held the attention of our craftsmen better than any scholar across the Dwarven clans. If they hear about even grander contraptions, they might just start a *Gutta'rhig,*" Erdueril chuckled.

"Gutta'rhig?"

"What did Alicia call it, a pilgrimage? A long journey of purpose, to gain knowledge and bring it back. Dwarven tradition, a proud and honored rite," Erdueril explained.

Alex laughed, "That's a long and *complicated* trip I'm afraid."

CHAPTER 27

After hours of driving, the cavern narrowed once again. Now on an incline, Alex was happy to see precious rays of daylight framing the transport ahead of them. She winced as the sun greeted her for the first time in days and she held a hand up to shield her eyes.

Cresting the slope, the war wagon pulled off to the right. Both of her team's buggies pulled off to the left, for a much-needed break. Alex got out and stretched, those tiny little vehicles were not designed for taller people.

"Well, thanks for getting us here Erdueril. I'm pretty confident we wouldn't have made it without you guys," Alex admitted.

Erdueril smiled and exited the transport, "It has been our pleasure. To make friends such as these, surface folk with such heart, it's a treasure worth the danger."

Alex smiled at his kind words, "I guess we'll have to come visit again."

Charlie walked up, "Heck yes we will. Dwarves are awesome, they just *get* me. You think I'm a dwarf boss? I'm pretty short."

Alex hadn't ever seen Charlie this energetic; it was both endearing and unnerving.

"You are an honorary one for certain!" Erdueril bellowed with a deep and hearty laugh.

"Best of luck with your trip, we'll be happy to see you again."

He gave Alex and Charlie a hug.

A while later, with the grinding of stone on stone, the entrance to the underground closed, leaving Alex and her team on their own once again.

"Fraygor."

"Alex?" Fraygor looked curious.

Alex checked her wrist computer, "How far are we from the capital?"

"Erdueril said this entrance was close to Widow's Rest, a settlement about two days' journey from the capital."

Alex furrowed her brow, "Any faster routes now that we've hopefully thrown the assassins off our trail?"

Fraygor pinched the bridge of his nose "I'm afraid not, the prince's chance at a punctual return is slim at this point," he grumbled.

Isaac asked, "It's not *that* big of a deal is it?"

"It is, Isaac. There is no telling what nonsense the court will conjure up to disparage the prince's reputation because of this," said Fraygor. "His enemies are not reasonable people, as you may have noticed from the multiple assassination attempts."

"You said two days' journey right?" asked Alex.

Fraygor nodded, "Yes, even with your transports. As impressive as they are, the dense forest between us and our destination will not allow them to move as fast as they usually do."

Isaac asked, "What about one of those?"

Alex turned to see him pointing at the river next to them. A decent-sized ship, a ferry of sorts, headed upstream.

"The river ramblers?" said Fraygor. "I suppose that would be faster since we are headed downstream, and it's a much more direct route."

"Where do those ferries leave from?" asked Alex.

"Widow's Rest, just ahead," said Calseous, despite the question being directed to Fraygor.

"Good thinking Isaac," Alex put her hand on his shoulder, "Let's get going."

It was a short drive, about fifteen minutes, but they had entered a thick tree line, much of the sun obscured by the canopy. It was hard to tell exactly where the town started, they had passed a few buildings here and there, but nothing particularly prominent.

Maybe Alex had been too hasty in calling Kairnos' town a hamlet. They passed by a few people carrying various goods, with more than a few odd looks at their transports.

"Not a lot of people here, are there Fraygor?" asked Alex.

"Widow's Rest is a sleepy town; I would say it's only even on a map because of the river rambler stop here."

Alex stifled a chuckle; she had been to more than a few towns on Earth that were like that.

"What's the story behind the name?" Alex was making conversation as their dull trip continued.

"Fairly simple, a few hundred years ago the town was started by a woman who couldn't bear to watch her husband die from disease. The legend goes that she ran away and wandered the woods for a week before finding this place and settling down. Depending on which version of the story you hear, the husband survived and never found his lost love."

Alex sensed a shift towards a more somber tone as he finished the story.

"You do so tell the history of our land rather well, Fraygor," said Calseous.

"Thank you, my liege."

Silence settled in as the buggies trudged along the rocky road, eventually coming to a fork.

Anthony was driving the vehicle ahead of them, and asked over the radio, "Which way?"

"If memory serves, it will be left," said Fraygor.

Alex slammed on the brakes when a cloaked figure sprawled across the hood of their vehicle with a thud.

Alex groaned, "You've got to be kidding me."

Another tussle with assassins.

Out of nowhere, a woman in green walked up and grabbed the cloaked person off their transport and tossed him to the ground.

They each drew blades, and in a flash there was an old-fashioned sword dual playing in front of them.

"Huh," Alex muttered as everyone watched the combat play out, "a fight that *doesn't* involve us. That's refreshing."

Over the clashing of steel on steel, Alex asked Calseous and Fraygor, "What's this about?"

Calseous shrugged, "I haven't the slightest clue."

Fraygor grumbled, got out of the vehicle, and drew his own sword. With a heavy upwards slice, Fraygor locked their blades disarming both combatants. The sheer force of his blow sent the weapons flying, shocking the two strangers.

Fraygor gritted his teeth, "Royal Guard, what is your quarrel?"

Now disarmed, Alex got a good look at the two. A boy, maybe sixteen years of age, wearing an unassuming and tattered cloak.

The other, a woman far better dressed. Her attire was made for combat, leather handguards, a dark green cloak, and a leather mask covering the lower half of her face.

Anger filled Fraygor and he repeated his question. In an instant the cloaked woman deftly swept the leg of the young man, sending him to the floor before she sprinted away.

Fraygor didn't give chase, instead opting to help the toppled boy off the ground. Alex and Calseous got out of the transport, the others still eying the spectacle from their seats.

Alex asked, "Why was she fighting you?"

The boy stood and briefly made eye contact before he looked behind him. "I'm…not sure. She just attacked me," he said sheepishly, "I really must be going, I was on my way to…"

A man's voice called, "Thief!"

An out of breath, portly, mustachioed man sprinted from behind a building. "That fool has taken my jewels!"

The young man bolted but Fraygor grabbed the boy's hood.

"It would seem you aren't being truthful with us," said Fraygor.

"A thief? How unruly!" said Calseous. He seemed aghast at the prospect.

Alex spotted a small hide sack the boy held firmly in one hand, tucked slightly within his cloak. She snatched it from him, feeling it's heft in her grip. She tossed the bag to the boy's accuser.

He opened it to reveal a small pile of large gems of various colors. "This criminal pilfered my entire stock, and just before I made it to market!" the man spat.

Dejected, the boy looked towards the ground, but did not utter a word.

"What do we do with him? Are there even guards in a little town like this?" Alex asked Fraygor.

"I'm afraid not, and we can't take him with us to the capital."

"Let me handle it," The voice came from above them.

Everyone looked up to see the green cloaked woman perched on a tree branch directly over them.

"My associates and I will deliver him to the nearest law keepers."

"As I thought, Arbiters," said Fraygor.

Alex locked her eyes on the armed woman. "Arbiters?"

"A group who have taken it upon themselves to serve justice to the lawless. They seem …dissatisfied with the crown's administration of the law." Fraygor shook his head.

Calseous gawked at the woman. "The Arbiters? I believed them to be a folk legend, some sort of urban fantasy to keep criminals on their toes."

"So, they're vigilantes?" asked Alex.

Fraygor furrowed his brow, “Alex, you know I have no idea what that means.”

Alex nodded, “Right.”

“Very well,” Fraygor said with a heavy sigh. “We’ll send him with you. We’ve no other options.”

The prince looked dumbfounded when the woman leapt from the tree and escorted the thief away.

“Are we just sending him away with those strangers? He is a criminal, yes, but surely his justice should be entrusted to someone more reputable?” Calseous argued.

“My liege, I admire your optimistic view of the world, but I’m afraid that in reality not every small hamlet has guards and a court to deal with each petty thief.” Fraygor walked back towards their transport.

“Then I will ensure that resources are allocated so that they do! It is ludicrous that some shadowy outlaws are the dispensers of justice!” the prince huffed.

Alex watched the woman disappear into the woods with her captive. She had a feeling that wouldn’t be the last time they dealt with these ‘Arbiters’.

Not long after their encounter, the team was waiting for the ferry.

Calseous and Fraygor were still arguing about whether sending the thief away was the right call, but that conversation was beginning to give Alex a headache.

Idle conversation was shared amongst the rest of them, so Alex opted to sit on the edge of the dock with her legs hanging off the end nearly touching the water.

Something had been nagging at her, ever since she had that nightmare.

What was with the Rifts? Their nature, their cause? It was an open-ended question, to be sure, and one that she was woefully unqualified to answer. Still, it weighed on her. It was their only way home, and she had no clue how they worked.

During their stay with the dwarves, it had occurred to her that no one had offered her an explanation for *why* the Rifts were opening.

Surely, if it had always happened, they would be known to humanity well before her time. The prevailing theory she had heard was that incursions from the Rifts were how much of the folklore and mythology in their respective locations on Earth was established, or at least influenced.

Still, if that was the case, why was there such a lapse between when those legends were written and the modern day? And more importantly, why only now were they opening again? Why had *their* Rift closed? Question after question swam in her head, and while she wanted to ask her science experts, she knew they had no more answers than she did.

The entire purpose of taking this prince to the capital was to find answers, but even that prospect wasn't exactly solid. She didn't know what to expect from the capital, it didn't sound like this court would be very helpful. Despite all the dangers they had faced up to this point, it was possible that political infighting would be their most daunting obstacle. On top of that, Alex wasn't thrilled at the prospect of sitting and waiting for others to act. If they *did* get help in the capital, it would probably take time, especially if bureaucracy was involved. Answers and solutions would come later. For now, she just had to focus on moving forward and keeping her team safe.

Alex looked back at them, smiling thankfully. She couldn't have done any of this without her team, even just the initial jump through the Rift. At every point she had relied on them, but more than that, they had grown from professional colleagues into something more.

Alex knew that she could count on each and every one of them at this point. Their bonds were forged not only in the literal heat of combat, but also by honesty and trust. It was different to the bonds she had in the military, more personal and sincere. It… *meant* more. She had realized this especially when Darius had been hurt, not only were they all concerned about him, but they all did what they could do to help.

As Alex reminisced, her eyes wandered from her team to her buggy. A door opened, and out stumbled a groggy Darius. Alex gasped, and her legs struggled to stand her up as quickly as her brain told them to.

She ran across to him but wasn't fast enough to arrive before he was swarmed by the others. A crying Alicia hugged him, Isaac grinned, and Anthony tried to focus on the area of his wound.

"We almost lost you!" Alicia sobbed.

Charlie was on her tiptoes, trying to get a word in.

It was Isaac's turn to hug, and Darius hugged him back. He smiled at his comrades but seemed confused.

"What exactly happened to me? I remember a sharp pain while we were driving but then nothing. How did we escape? When did we get out of the underground? Wait, How long have I been out?"

"The dwarves saved us," said Charlie.

Isaac released his hug, "And then Anthony and the dwarf doctors fixed you up."

"It was a pretty close call," Anthony admitted, "I'm just glad you're okay."

"I missed the dwarves?" Darius seemed disappointed but that didn't disrupt his smile.

"They were awesome!" Charlie proceeded to ramble on about the magnetic ore.

Each of the team shared about their experiences with the dwarves, poor Darius absolutely flooded with stories and anecdotes. By the look on his face Alex could tell he wouldn't want to be anywhere else.

Darius struggled to keep up, until he suddenly locked eyes with her. The rest of them continued on, interrupting one another, but for a brief moment Alex and Darius held eye contact.

Darius gave her a firm nod, and a notably different smile. Alex nodded back, it was the unspoken stuff she wasn't usually good at, but the message got across to her just fine in this instance.

Darius was happy to be home.

The group chatted until the ferry arrived about an hour later. After a brief exchange with the captain, he cautiously agreed to *try* to load the buggies onto the vessel.

Mooring the ship as close to the dock as possible, Anthony and Isaac carefully maneuvered their vehicles aboard. The ferry was apparently used to carrying wagons and carts, but the buggies, Alex surmised, would be heavier.

With a few creaks, the ferry tilted, but the vessel accepted its bizarre cargo. With a sigh of relief, Alex boarded alongside the others.

It was starting to get dark by the time they had finally made it aboard. Alex had lost much of her sense of time during their adventure underground, so despite the encroaching darkness she wasn't very tired.

Alicia, Darius, and Fraygor on the other hand, were all tired. Darius and Fraygor were still in pretty rough shape, and Alicia was still behind on sleep. Anthony sat by Darius, monitoring his patient as he slept.

Isaac stood on the bow of the ship. Alex had asked him to keep watch, but she suspected he was more interested in the stars than any potential dangers.

Calseous sat in one of the few interior portions of the ships, his head down and his shoulders slumped. Alex had hardly even thought of the prince since they entered the underground, and after their conversation in the tavern she was feeling a bit guilty for that. She had been focused, rightfully so, on her team. But still, seeing him the way he was now, and how upset he got about the thief and the Arbiters, Alex decided to talk to him.

Taking a makeshift seat on a crate across from him, Alex asked, "How are you holding up?"

"Pardon?" Calseous looked confused.

"Holding up, it's an Earth expression. How are you handling things? How are you doing?" she explained.

"I see. Well, I am afraid my ability to hold things up is waning. I grow weary of travel and danger. What's more, seeing the cracks and flaws of our nation up close,...it is more than slightly disheartening" The prince avoided eye contact.

Alex hesitated; she knew what she *wanted* to say but wasn't sure how he would take it.

"Can I be honest Calseous?"

"Prince Calseous..." he corrected but sounded defeated.

"Calseous, listen. I appreciate your optimism and that you see the best in people, but sometimes you need to be realistic about how bad things are before you can make it better."

Calseous briefly looked up at her, before returning his gaze to the floor. "I suppose there is wisdom in that."

They were both quiet, only the sound of the river flowing around their transport.

"That night in the woods..." she reluctantly began, "I told you about my...hardship."

Calseous looked up with a raised brow, but he didn't interrupt.

"I know I said that it meant nothing, that we'd never meet again. Obviously I was wrong, about both of those."

"How so?" Calseous asked after a brief pause.

"Well, I was wrong that we'd never meet again, look where we are now. But I was also wrong that it meant nothing to me. I was upset when I found out you lied about being the prince, about your situation. I wouldn't have been mad if I hadn't been...vulnerable."

"I see. Then, are you still angry with me?"

Alex shook her head, "Not anymore. All of that led to me opening up to my team, and I don't think we would have made it this far if not for the bond that we fostered."

Calseous' expression shifted to a slight smile.

Alex felt self-conscious about the subject matter, and she looked away. "I'm not the best at this stuff. I'm more the introspective type, not usually up for sharing what I'm thinking, or how I feel."

"I had gathered that."

Alex's face melted into a smile. "I guess what I'm saying is… thank you. You let me vent when I needed to, and you gave me the chance to be honest with my people."

Calseous looked a bit surprised, shocked almost.

"I never told a soul you know, not even Fraygor. And I was going to tell you, that I was the prince, I mean. I am afraid our encounter with my former guard squandered that moment."

Alex smiled, "I appreciate the honesty, even if you didn't get a chance to express it."

She had wandered into this open conversation without even realizing it. What's more, she was comfortable in it. As annoying as she sometimes found the prince, he was easy to talk to in a certain way. He walked a fine line between optimism and naivety, but his struggle to navigate that line was a bit endearing.

The two of them sat in the quiet dark, the flickering light of candles the only illumination.

Calseous cleared his throat and stood, "I believe it is time for some sleep. We arrive at the capital in the morning."

"True. Gotta say, I'm not looking forward to a sleeping bag on wooden planks. Please tell me they have comfortable beds in the capital?" Alex laughed.

"The best, well, to my knowledge at least. Based on his demeanor in the morning I've long suspected Fraygor's bed to be subpar compared to my own."

Alex laughed. A joke from the prince? That was a first.

Calseous smiled at her, "Good night Miss Alex."

She returned the smile, and as the young prince walked away, Alex felt at ease. Maybe things really were going to be okay.

CHAPTER 28

"BOSS, WAKE UP!" Isaac said.

"Huh?"

"You're gonna want to see this," Isaac ran outside.

Alex got up and followed him.

She left the dimly lit cabin and stepped onto the ship's deck. The glaring sun temporarily blinded her, and she raised a hand to shield her eyes.

She was immediately engrossed in what Isaac was so excited about. Beyond the dock was a sinkhole, easily a mile wide.

She jumped off the dock with Isaac and they hurried over to the rest of her team who stared at a city within the massive hole. The terrain was split into multiple concentric rings, every one covered with buildings, and the levels descended each lower than the last. A massive white tower at the deepest part of the pit was so tall it rose out of the center of the sinkhole.

From that tower extended four massive bridges, flat on the top and arched at the bottom. Waterfalls dotted the rim of the circular cliffside and about a dozen rivers meandered through the city, all appearing to end at the central tower.

"Welcome to Kestalvier, the city in the ground," Fraygor said proudly.

"Oh, I hate when people call it that, it makes it sound like we live in the dirt!" Calseous said.

"Kestalvier is a proud and ancient city Fraygor, we must give it the respect it deserves."

Alex wasn't sure what she had been expecting, the journey here had been far too eventful to leave her time or energy to ponder what the capital looked like. Even still, the sight before her was nowhere near what her guess would have been.

"I have…so many questions," Alex said to nobody in particular.

Fraygor smirked, "Then, my liege, as I leave to arrange transport to the city center, I trust you will introduce our guests to our home?"

She looked at the prince, he seemed shocked.

"He *never* leaves me alone. He must truly trust you, Miss Alex."

Alex smiled and shrugged and turned back to the immense city. "How are we getting down into the city? I'm guessing you don't have elevators?" Alex said, knowing that the word could be lost in translation.

"We have the risers if that is what you mean. But we will not need to take one of those till we make it to the spire," Calseous acted as though she should already know this.

"Spire? You mean the big tower in the middle?" asked Isaac.

"Precisely Mister Isaac! We will take the bridges to the spire and *then* we will descend directly to the court chambers."

Charlie asked, "Will we be able to take the buggies?"

"I do not see why not, there are carriages on the bridge spans each and every day."

Calseous answered question after question, but the conversation blurred into the background noise as Alex's mind wandered.

Would they really get any help from this court? Even if they could help them, would they be willing to? How involved would they need to get, and could they afford to? What about the prince? Would Calseous be any safer here than he was on the road?

She sighed. The prince wasn't her responsibility, she had to focus on her people. But in the back of her mind, it still nagged at her.

Darius interrupted her thoughts, "Alex, we're ready to leave."

Alex nodded. Having just woken up she still felt tired.

The team carefully unloaded the buggies from the ferry. It was just as delicate as loading. The boat raised in the water as the excess weight was released, and the ferry captain seemed relieved when Fraygor handed him their payment for the trip.

Unlike Caltesia, they got strange looks for their transport from almost every person they passed. When they slowly drove through a massive gate that led them onto the nearest bridge, Alex saw a waterway flowing across the bridge.

"The water flows out of the spire?"

"Oh yes, the rivers flow into the city, terminating at the spire. From there the water is lifted to the surface and sent out via the aqueducts," said an enthusiastic Calseous.

Alex looked at the manmade river, "Lifted *how*?"

"Some magical means that I myself do not entirely understand. You should listen to Aluwain speak on the subject; she could talk about it for hours without stopping for so much as a breath!"

Alex felt her stomach lurch when she looked at the city below them. It was always an ironic thing for her, she had no fear of heights when it came to flying but being on top of tall buildings,...that was something else.

They passed by several wagons, carts, even fancy carriages as they drove across the considerably long bridge. Finally, they entered the part of the structure where all of the bridges met, near the tip of the spire. The interior was a massive circular hall, the majority of which seemed to be taken up by wagons unloading goods.

Fraygor directed Isaac to a suitable parking spot, and Alex could feel the curious gazes of everyone within line of sight as they brought their *steel carriages* to a halt. They got out, and Alex was happy to see that their clothes still let them blend in. In fact, much better it seemed than the people exiting the carriage nearest to them.

A man and a woman, both regally dressed, curiously eyed Alex and her group.

The woman shouted, “Is that? It is! Prince Calseous!”

“Councilor Zalta!” Calseous said to the man.

The woman walked straight past Alex, as though she weren’t there, and directly to the prince.

“We had heard such terrible rumors, that you had been kidnapped or even worse!” The woman’s regal tone and cadence matching Calseous’.

A middle-aged man nonchalantly walked past Alex.

He said to Calseous, “Aluwain has been worried sick.” The man glanced around, casting a cautious look towards Alex. “And where are your guards? I see Sir Fraygor is still accompanying you, but I don’t recognize any of these—others.”

Fraygor said, “It has been a complicated journey. I appreciate your concern for his highness’ safety, but we must be getting to the court now.”

“Nonsense Fraygor, we can surely stop to speak for a bit,” Calseous insisted.

“*My liege…*” Fraygor grumbled.

Calseous relented, “I suppose he is right. Another time my friends, I shall see you in the court?”

“Very well,” the Councilor said. “However, do be careful of Councilor Aldron. He has been upset, dare I say livid, with your extended absence.”

“So good to see you,” The woman said as the pair walked away.

“Friends of yours?” Darius asked as he unloaded the vehicles.

“The Zaltas. Some of the few on the council I can truly call friends. Their daughter, Aluwain, is my closest advisor, after Fraygor of course.”

Alex was glad to see not everyone hated the prince, that was the impression she got from what Fraygor had been saying.

"Let's leave whatever we don't need right now, we can come get it later. "Alex said to her team before turning to Fraygor, "Is there somewhere we can stay?"

As he often did, Fraygor stroked his stubble. "There are many rooms for guests in the court portion of the spire, but I would prefer you to stay in the royal guard barracks, it will be closer to the prince *and* the king should problems arise."

Alex nodded, "Well then, let's get you to court Calseous," she turned to see him already walking away.

"*Prince* Calseous!" he pointed his finger in the air as if to correct her.

Oh boy, they're not all going to be like him, are they?

CHAPTER 29

After a few turns down a couple of hallways, they were greeted by an empty room that seemingly led nowhere. Still, Fraygor and Calseous entered, and after the team shared some confused looks, they followed them inside. Suddenly the room shook, and the hallway behind them jolted upwards, they were going down. Alongside the occasional rumble, there was a slight humming noise.

"Risers," said Calseous. "I'll bet that you do not have *these* where you come from! They are powered by runic magic!"

Sure enough, on the sides of the riser were runic symbols, but different from the dwarven ones they had seen earlier.

These glowed a purple-ish blue, and the symbols were smoother, with more curves, and less angles than the dwarf ones. The rune symbol repeated over and over as they descended but were different on each side.

They suddenly jolted to a stop. Curiously, Alex didn't feel that sense of movement or inertia the entire time they had been moving, more magic she supposed.

Stepping off the riser, they entered a maze of hallways with a *lot* of ornate white marble staircases, to the point that Alex questioned why they had the elevator at all. They descended one final set of steps, approaching a grand door.

It was almost comically tall, like an indoor gate, but intricately decorated, like everything else since the riser. On either side of the door were armored guards, in full helmets that obscured their faces. They held greatswords, similar to Fraygor's.

Calseous stopped ahead of the guards, and turned to Alex, "Miss Alex, I am afraid I must ask your companions to wait here. I am already barging in late and unannounced; I would not like to cause a scene with a whole gaggle of armed foreigners as well."

Alex turned to her team. A nod from Darius, a shrug from Charlie, and a frown from Isaac. Mixed feelings all around.

Fraygor and Calseous approached the door, Alex following suit. The two guards moved to open the door, each impressively holding their swords aloft with their free hand. A bright light shone through the door as it opened, and Alex shielded her eyes as she crossed the threshold of the court. She could hear echoes of voices as she entered the immense chamber.

It resembled a concert hall, albeit a small one, nearly forming a full semi-circle. In place of rows of seats, were a number of ornate wooden desks, evenly spaced from one another. Most were occupied. A woman in regal dress stood at a podium in the front of the room. Behind her, a massive cylinder of flowing water.

The vertical aqueduct.

The woman was saying, "We cannot simply allow outlaws to dispense justice however they see fit. It places distrust in the hearts of each and every subject of our kingdom."

A man behind one of the desks responded, "Then what do you suggest we do, councilor? Send a guard regiment to each and every miniscule village in the nation? How would we pay for such a thing? The tax is high as it is."

Calseous cleared his throat, "Esteemed Councilors! I have returned. I must apologize for my absence, I'm afraid I have troubled news."

A loud voice bellowed, "Prince Calseous. How gracious of you to interrupt us, and only *three days* late."

Calseous frowned, "Councilor Aldron, I apologize profusely for my tardiness, but I assure you it was beyond my control."

Another councilor seemed to be heckling the prince. "As are many things, young prince. It seems you've an excuse for every blunder. Tell me, what damage have you done to our relationship with our neighbors to the west?"

"There are more pressing matters, I assure you," Calseous insisted.

Yet another voice rang out, sending the entire council chamber into uproar. "More pressing matters than our security? I would think not."

Calseous' shoulders slumped with each insult flung at him. He seemed to have some supporters, but their comments could not be heard.

Alex watched Fraygor scowl in silence; she felt the same. She had expected dysfunction, but not the sheer vitriol she was witnessing now. As the arguing reached a fever pitch, Alex couldn't take it any longer and stepped forward, past the Prince.

Standing nearly in the center of the room, Alex shouted at the top of her lungs.

"Hey! Listen to what he has to say!" her voice echoing through the room.

There was a deafening silence, and *all* eyes were on her, a sensation that would have normally made Alex uncomfortable were she not so frustrated.

The one Calseous had called Aldron said, "Who in the blazes are you?"

Alex shouted so that she could be heard, but quieter and less angry this time. "Alexandria Petrakis, I met your prince on his journey back."

"And for what reason should we listen to you?" Aldron hissed.

Alex tried to keep from scowling at the man, "You shouldn't, you should listen to Calseous, I'm sure he wants to tell you about the multiple assassination attempts that we've dealt with on the way here."

Aldron looked at the prince skeptically, and low murmurs rumbled through the crowd.

"Very well. Prince Calseous, speak your part," said Aldron.

"Thank you councilor," Calseous began fervently, "As Miss Alex has said, there were several attempts on my life. Many of my guards were slain in the process of protecting me. Most troubling of all, one member of the royal guard attempted to assassinate me herself!"

Gasps were heard throughout the room, and the murmuring grew louder and more urgent.

"Silence!" Aldron bellowed, and the room quieted instantly.

The woman at the podium asked indignantly, "We are to believe that a member of the royal guard, the most elite and trusted of our military, tried to kill the very man they were sworn to protect?"

"If this is true it is most troubling," another councilor admitted.

"Of course it isn't true! Young Calseous is simply telling stories again," another laughed, a small group joining in.

Fraygor took off his cloak and handed it to Alex, then he stepped forward. His shirt still had the scorch mark from the magical projectile he took, and through a hole in the shoulder his large wound was clearly visible.

"One group of assassins who attacked us in Caltesia left this present on my shoulder," he displayed it for the entire room. "They wielded magic and wore strange white masks."

"We had to travel in the dwarven underground just to avoid them," Alex scanned across the room as the councilors discussed with each other in hushed voices.

A councilwoman shouted, "An investigation must be conducted!"

"Very well," Aldron once again silenced the room. "We will allocate resources to investigate whether these bold claims are true."

Alex smirked, finally they were getting somewhere.

The woman at the podium proclaimed, "A waste of time and resources. Mysterious magical assassins, traitors in the royal guard, *dwarves* beneath our kingdom. This sounds like a fairy tale."

Another councilor stood up to interject, "How do you explain Captain Fraygor's wound? The captain of the royal guard would not simply lie, let alone before the court."

Alex handed Fraygor his cloak as the room broke into shouting.

"Order!" Aldron bellowed, "I'm cutting this session short, clearly you all need to cool your heads before we make *any* decisions."

Aldron descended the steps and walked directly past the prince.

Calseous sheepishly walked up to Alex and Fraygor, and as the courtroom began to empty, Fraygor let out a frustrated sigh.

"How convenient, a matter as important as attempted murder of the monarchy is postponed," he shook his head.

Alex couldn't help but share his cynicism. Her introduction to the court hadn't exactly gone well, and they didn't even get a chance to talk about the rifts.

Calseous looked more dejected than ever, and Alex couldn't blame him. She never really treated him any different for being a prince, but the court seemed to hate him for it. She was debating if she should say something when she saw a young woman approaching them.

"Calseous, thank goodness you're alright!" She put both hands on his shoulders.

"Aluwain, it is wonderful to see you, although I must disagree that I am alright." Calseous was clearly happy to see his friend, but it did little to pull him out of his melancholy.

"Oh, that Aldron, and councilor Gyld as well! They treat you so poorly," said Aluwain.

Calseous did his best to straighten his posture. "Ah, Miss Alex, this is Aluwain. The court mage and head magical advisor to the throne."

"Pleased to meet you," the young woman said, performing a sort of curtsy.

"Likewise," said Alex, slightly confused at the gesture, "That's an impressive set of titles for someone so young." Alex guessed she couldn't be any more than twenty years old.

Aluwain was relatively short; freckles sprinkled her pale complexion, short black messy hair sticking out on the sides and glasses that framed her brown eyes.

She wore a far less elegant outfit than the councilors. Instead, she had a neatly tucked blouse with a large purple cloak around her shoulders. Curiously, she wore some oversized leather gloves on her hands.

"Thank you!" said Aluwain. "Although, I must admit I would not be anywhere without the prince's advocacy."

"Oh Aluwain, you flatter me," Calseous said with a cheerier tone.

With wide inquisitive eyes, Aluwain said, "Tell me then, who is your new friend? Miss Alex was it?"

"Just Alex is fine."

"Oh, an informal one, I admire that. Where are you from, Alex?"

Alex and Calseous shared a concerned glance, but Alex figured that if the court mage was going to help them solve the riddle of the rifts, she ought to know the whole story.

"Well, do you want the short answer or the long one?" Alex joked.

Aluwain looked up, as if in deep thought, "Hmm, I would say the short answer now and the long answer when you've more time."

Taking a deep breath and stealing her nerves, Alex quickly explained. "My friends and I are from a world called Earth. We came here through a sort of portal thing we call the 'Rift', but it closed and now we're stranded here."

Aluwain's eyes practically glimmered, "Fascinating, the longer version please."

Fraygor gestured towards the door. "I'm afraid we've no time for that, we must see the king." He directed everyone to begin walking.

Sensing Aluwain wanted more answers, Alex said, "You know, I have a friend who'd *love* to talk to you."

They exited the courtroom, where Alex saw Isaac standing in front of one of the stoic guards by the door. With a hand on his chin, Isaac squinted and leaned in close to the armored soldier.

"Do you think they're statues?" asked Isaac not taking his eyes off the guard.

"Isaac, we saw them move earlier, remember?" said Anthony.

Isaac narrowed his eyes more. "*Magic* statues."

Alex snickered slightly at the display before hearing Charlie approach her.

"Well, boss? How did it go?" asked Charlie.

"Not great, we didn't even get a chance to bring up our situation, and they basically just ragged on the prince the whole time," Alex whispered.

"Alex, I have so many questions about the court! How does this sort of governing system work? The cultural implications alone," Alicia was obviously excited.

"Actually, Alicia," Alex gestured towards Aluwain. "Our new friend here has her own questions about us. You two should talk."

Aluwain joined them. "Oh, there are more of you, this is fantastic."

She addressed Alex's entire team, "Aluwain Zalta, court mage and chief magical advisor to the crown."

Isaac's eyes lit up, "Magic? Like, *magic* magic?"

Aluwain looked puzzled, "Is…there a kind of non-magical magic?"

Charlie snickered and looked Aluwain up and down. "I'd say

we've got some pretty magical things that don't use a lick of magic."

Aluwain gasped, "I must speak with you, all of you." She looked at Alex, as though asking permission.

Alex turned to Fraygor and Calseous. Do you guys need me from here?"

"I do not think so," Calseous said, before his expression changed to one of realization. "Oh! Miss Alex, you must meet my father. Afterwards you may speak with Aluwain as long as you wish."

Fraygor seemed uncomfortable.

Alex said, "Alicia, you go talk with Aluwain; learn what you can and explain our situation. Tell her everything, I think we're past keeping a low profile and hiding our origins at this point."

Alicia nodded eagerly at Aluwain, "Shall we?" The two walked away.

Close behind, Isaac followed the two women, "Can I come?"

Alex laughed and shook her head. Isaac seemed like a tourist sometimes.

"You guys settle in, get our equipment off the buggies. Where was that guard barracks, Fraygor?" asked Alex.

Fraygor called over to one of the guards by the door, "Find our guests some bunks in the guard quarters," he ordered.

The armored guard nodded, his metal helmet shifting and making a slight grinding noise.

As the guard led the rest of her team away, Alex and Calseous followed Fraygor up a different set of stairs. It was time to meet a king.

At the top of the stairs, they took a riser and Alex felt a slight rumble when it stopped. This one had taken them much higher than the previous one had.

The entrance to the room ahead of them opened on its own, and the prince stepped in first. Fraygor and Alex followed, while guards held the doors open. They walked down a long hallway and through a much larger and grander door.

The entire chamber had a certain sheen to it from the polished stone surfaces, and the white marble motif seemed to be popular here. When Alex walked through the door she noticed the guards on either side of the corridor. She thought they looked like the court guards, but with far more ornate armor.

Alex could see her reflection in the warped gold-like material of their exquisitely polished platemail. A single guard stood before the large doors at the end of the hallway, and as they approached him, Calseous gave him one of his strange 'special salutes'. Alex had meant to ask him about those, and why his was different. The guard returned a different salute, the one she had seen both Fraygor and Kairnos flash a while back.

Calseous said in a formal tone, "Greetings, Sir Knight, I wish to see the king."

In a deep, stoic voice the guard said, "I'm afraid you are not permitted to enter the king's chambers at this time, my liege."

Calseous looked surprised, but Fraygor rushed forward. "By whose orders? I haven't even been here!" he growled.

"The king's order, Captain," the guard's voice cracked.

Fraygor scowled and clenched his fist. He looked like he was going to say something, but he shrugged and turned to Calseous. "I'm sorry my liege, there is nothing I can do."

"But my father…" Calseous began, but Fraygor cut him off.

"Calseous, we must go," the older man said solemnly.

The prince looked bewildered. He sighed and walked away.

Alex and Fraygor followed him.

Fraygor gave her a subtle bump with his elbow, and whispered, "The last time I saw the king, he was too ill to speak, much less give orders. Some snake on the court is preventing Calseous from seeing his father."

Alex thought for a moment, "If they're doing something that blatant they must be planning for something to happen *soon.*"

"My exact worry Alex. They could make their move at any

time. however,...I have some ideas what their exact goal is, but it'll take some looking into."

Alex raised an eyebrow, "Meaning?"

"I need you to protect Calseous while I get to the bottom of this."

"What?" Alex stopped, her surprise betraying her as she spoke a bit too loudly.

"Miss Alex? Fraygor?" Calseous stopped too and faced them. "What is the matter?"

Fraygor shot Alex a sideways glance, before returning his attention to Calseous and clearing his throat.

"My liege, there are matters I must attend to. I will leave you in Miss Alex's capable hands."

Calseous looked at him, with a blank expression, "Very well, Fraygor."

Fraygor started to walk away but stopped and glanced back; the prince was looking at the floor. He finally looked up and quickly Fraygor left.

CHAPTER 30

CALSEOUS LED ALEX to Aluwain's study, she was starting to realize that this tower was one giant vertical maze with far too many sets of stairs. Walking alongside the prince, Alex couldn't help but feel sad for him, but also a bit mad at Fraygor.

Not only had he just dropped the duty of being Calseous' bodyguard on her out of nowhere, but he also left immediately. The poor prince must surely have felt a bit cast aside, between not being able to see his father and Fraygor *literally* abandoning him.

She couldn't really think of what to say to Calseous, so she figured the best thing she could do for him right now was to follow Fraygor's orders.

After descending on one of the risers, they exited onto a dimly lit floor lined with bricks made of some darker stone, possibly granite, a stark contrast to the marble of the rest of the tower.

She looked around, "This is very different."

Calseous smiled, "The mages do like their atmospheric lighting".

They walked through an open, thick wooden door to find Alicia and Isaac, sitting on the floor with Aluwain. Papers, books, and Alicia's tablet were sprawled out between them.

Her study was rather large for a single person but that was mostly due to the wall of tall bookcases.

A few things caught Alex's eye. In the center of the room was a floating series of objects that almost looked like a clock or a compass. Multiple pointed brass pieces rotated around the slightly glowing center. To the right of that, near Aluwain, was an immense wooden desk covered in a chaotic array of papers and books. The long wooden staff that leaned against it had a purple-ish blue crystal adorning the tip and was almost as tall as Alex.

Alicia was saying, “And this is where we entered our side of the Rift.” She pointed to the screen of her tablet.

“Fascinating. So, it *does* line up,” Aluwain exclaimed.

Isaac looked up, “Boss, you gotta see all this, it’s amazing. She’s got all sorts of magic stuff, and *she’s* magic. She made fire with her hands.”

Aluwain blushed slightly, “It’s not a particularly difficult spell Isaac.”

“As impressive as it *was*,” Alicia began, “I think Alex needs to hear about some other more pressing discoveries.” She patted the floor next to her, and Calseous sat between Alicia and Aluwain.

Alex looked around.

There’s chairs in the room.

She shrugged, and then she sat down.

Alicia held up the tablet screen so that Alex could see it. On it was displayed a map of the European continent on Earth. “What does this look like to you?” Alicia asked with a grin.

“Europe? Why?”

Alicia tapped on an icon on the display and suddenly the borders of the map were different. More curious than that, text was now displayed, labeling the revised borders.

Alex squinted, “Kresgroh, Caltesia, Kestalvier…” she muttered. Her eyes widened and she looked at Alicia. “No way.”

“It’s parallel Alex!” Alicia beamed, “The entire world!”

“Well, close to parallel, yes. It seems that when you left Switzerland, you arrived near Kresgroh, and those spots lined up perfectly on both the map of our world, Vertos, and yours, Earth," Aluwain explained.

"So, let me get this straight, any time a rift opens on Earth, it leads to the parallel spot on this planet?" Alex asked, still taking in this new information.

"Precisely!" said Alicia.

"But…our Rift was inside a mountain, how on earth did that lead to a field on the other side if they're parallel?" asked Alex.

"Well, it doesn't seem to be *identical*," Aluwain pointed out. "The topology is different, mountains and rivers in different places, but the continents seem to line up."

Alex wasn't sure if this was a ridiculously big deal right now or not, it might just be something for Alicia and Anthony to drool over, but at the same time it *could* lead them to answers about the Rifts.

"What about the Rifts themselves? Any news on that?" she asked.

Alicia and Aluwain both frowned.

"There's a bit of a hitch with that one, Alex," said Alicia.

"I have never heard of such a thing in any of my tomes. If Alicia's theory about your world's mythology is correct, it would have been about a thousand years ago that the last Rifts were open. If that lines up with the Rifts in Vertos, the last records of them here would be in the ancient archives from that same time period," said Aluwain.

"So…what's the problem? Just check those archives," said Alex.

Aluwain sighed, "It's not that simple, unfortunately, anything that goes back further than three hundred years is sealed away, only accessible if you have a missive from the court granting permission. They will not allow us to search the archives, not even the court mage, without good reason and approval."

"And since the prince has enemies on the court, that's going to be difficult to pull off," observed Alex.

Aluwain looked at Calseous with a frown, "Unfortunately, yes."

Thoughtfully, Alex twisted her mouth. She knew that the specter of bureaucracy would rear its ugly head at some point.

"However," Aluwain began, "If you can round up enough support from the court, we can get approval. A majority would seal the deal, and the prince *does* have a favorable reputation with many on the court. It's just dealing with those in the middle ground that I'm worried about."

Calseous plopped his chin in his hand. "This is a predicament to be sure."

Alex said, "Snooping around for votes could have the unintended side-effect of speeding along the plans of Calseous' assassins. If they see he's rallying support, they could move to kill him again. Especially if he's successful."

There was a brief silence, before Isaac said, "Wait, Aluwain, what about the party?"

"The 'masquerade'?"

"Party?" said Alex.

Aluwain nodded, "Yes, the entire court will be there. It's an annual event to celebrate the beginning of court sessions. My father is hosting it this year in fact. Oh Isaac, that's brilliant!"

"Okay, guys, what's brilliant?" asked Alex.

"Everyone will be in one place at the same time, so we can wine and dine them all at once. Get support in a few hours, quicker than Calseous' enemies can figure out what we're doing," said Isaac.

Alex looked at Isaac and squinted, "I'm thinking."

It was a risky plan, to rile up the prince's would-be killers, but if they got enough support from others on the court, it could also move along the investigation to the assassination attempts. That would definitely put their enemies on the defensive.

Finally, she said, "I like this idea, Isaac. Aluwain, tell me more about this party. You said it's a masquerade? How do you even know that word?"

Aluwain's eyes lit up, "Alicia taught me. We call it a Sekouri here, but the idea of wearing whimsical masks to the party is very similar. It's happening tonight."

Alex smiled, Aluwain reminded her a bit of Isaac; young and eager.

She said, "Great, so we all head to the party, get people on his side for both the archive access *and* the investigation. This sounds like a good plan."

Aluwain shook her head. "Oh dear, Alex. No, you seem to misunderstand. Only members of the court may attend the party. I'm afraid Prince Calseous and I will need to do this on our own."

There it was—the complication. In their time here, that always seemed to arise in an otherwise solid plan.

Alex sighed, she didn't like the idea of Calseous in there alone, especially with Fraygor having *just* entrusted him to her. "Isn't there going to be security or something? Can I go in there with him?"

Aluwain winced, "The court sees no need for security within the dining hall itself, I daresay they are used to the luxury of not being targets for assassination."

There was a pause as everyone seemed lost in thought, looking for a solution. Alex saw a look of realization on Calseous' face, followed by a slightly sheepish glance towards her.

"There is…one way," he said with hesitation.

Alex raised an eyebrow, "What?"

"Court members are the primary guests, but they are each allowed to bring a guest of their own, usually a spouse or…"

Alex scowled, "Don't say date."

"Very well, if not a date, then an escort?" he asked.

"Nope," Alex shot back.

"...Accompaniment?" Calseous offered.

Alex let out a long, defeated sigh, mixed with a bit of a grumble. "Let me guess," she muttered, "Formal dress?"

"But of course, it is a party after all!" Calseous laughed.

Isaac looked away, awkwardly rubbing the back of his neck, while Alicia did a poor job of holding back an amused smile.

Aluwain blushed.

"Fine," Alex said, "I'll be your *accompaniment*, but only undercover as your bodyguard."

"Of course, Miss Alex! Oh, this shall be so daring, keeping secrets at a party, like one of those drama performances Fraygor used to take me to. Deception, espionage, intrigue!" Calseous was more than excited.

Oh boy. This is going to be a long night.

CHAPTER 31

ALEX GLARED at Charlie and Alicia, who couldn't hold back grins. The past hour had been a flurry of clothing options, and Alex hated every second of it. Now she was being fitted for a dress, which her '*friends*' apparently found hilarious.

The tailor, a woman old enough to be her grandmother, was trying to help her, "How much more of this do I have to endure?"

She measured her sides, "Just a bit more, now raise your arms dearie."

Alex begrudgingly held her arms up straight. To say she was uncomfortable would be a massive understatement, and she continued to give her teammates a dirty look.

"After this, we'll do makeup," Alicia giggled.

"Yeah boss, you're gonna look *hot*," Charlie joked, as she sat back in a chair.

Alex gritted her teeth, "I hate you guys."

At least it was just these two, Alicia had banished the boys.

Alex said, "Let's go through the plan again."

"Right. You'll go in, protect the prince, and we'll keep an eye out for any bad guys. I'll be in your earpiece the whole time, so if you need any date advice just ask me." Charlie chuckled.

"It's not a date!" Alex growled, "It's a mission. Besides, you don't seem like the dating type, Charlie."

"You kiddin'? I had boys falling all over me in college. I went on a few pity dates but honestly never met anyone there that I found interesting."

"Wait, really?" Alicia looked skeptical.

"Yep. Full on man magnet right here," Charlie proclaimed. She tapped her chest with her thumbs. "Although to be fair, I was one of like only three girls at an engineering school."

"I guess we had different experiences. I met Anthony and we've been dating ever since. I've never dated anyone else," said Alicia.

The tailor pushed Alex's arms down and moved to measure her back.

"What about you, Alex?" Alicia asked.

Alex's scowl transitioned to annoyance. "I've…never been on a real date before," she admitted.

Alicia and Charlie's amused smiles disappeared as their eyes widened. The two women shared a sideways glance.

Alicia said, "Like, *never* never?"

Alex shook her head, "Nope. Not anything I would qualify as a date at least."

"Have you ever tried?" Charlie asked flatly.

"*Charlie!*" Alicia jabbed Charlie with her elbow.

Alex shrugged. *It was a fair question.*

"A few times, well, okay *one* time," Alex admitted. "In high-school, senior year, I was getting teased like crazy for never having gone to any of the dances. So, I figured 'I'll show them. I'll get all dolled up and I'll go ask *Mitch Douglas* to the big fall formal dance.'"

"Let me guess, the *dreamiest guy in school,* according to all the other girls?" Alicia smiled.

"Big time."

"So…what happened?" asked Charlie.

Alex sighed, she had shared more serious stuff with them than this, just not as embarrassing.

"I walked up to him after school, did my best to be cute or whatever, and he..."

"He what?" Alicia and Charlie said in unison, hanging on every word.

"He said he couldn't dance with someone so much taller than him. Said he didn't think he could reach my shoulder."

"How short *was* this dude?" asked Charlie.

"Not short enough for that to be a *real* issue, but he said it loud enough for the whole hallway to hear, and I was basically laughed out of the building."

Alicia's eyes were misty, "Oh Alex, that's terrible,"

Alex had basically put romance to the backburner after that, focusing on her career instead. Apart from that experience the one or two minor crushes she had growing up were her only other glimpses of the dating world.

"I must admit, Miss," the tailor said, shaking Alex from her stupor, "You are quite tall for a lady."

Alex grimaced, "Thanks."

The tailor said, "I mean no offense dear. I find it an exciting challenge of my skills. I am used to short and dainty ladies in this place, so to make a dress for a tall and strong woman like you is a pleasant departure from the standard."

Alicia saw Alex's discomfort and stood, "It'll be fine. Like you said, it's not even a real date!"

"Well, I mean, she *does* sort of need to be convincing," Charlie pointed out.

"*Charlie...*" Alicia chided.

Alex sighed, "No, she's right. If I'm the obvious replacement bodyguard no one will talk to us. I have to be as polite and disarming as possible."

"So, what are we gonna do? No offense, boss but you ain't exactly the laid-back girly girl type, that's more Alicia's deal," said Charlie.

Alex wasn't sure how to answer the question, and Charlie was right. Alex had never seen herself as a tomboy or anything like that, but she certainly didn't fit into the more standard *girly girl* category Alicia resided in.

"It's only for a few hours, you can fake it for that long, right?" asked Alicia.

Before Alex could respond, the tailor said, "Alright dear, that should be all I need. Is there anything else you'd like to try on?"

Alex looked around the room, her eyes settling on a bizarre looking piece of clothing.

"What's that weird belt—vest thingy?"

"Alex, that's a corset," Alicia grinned.

"I'll take that. It's the closest thing I'm gonna get to armor or some sort of protection."

"Okay," Alicia let out a soft sigh. "Maybe she can't fake it."

Alex, in her full party getup; the dress, corset, and makeup included, walked down the halls of the spire with Charlie and Alisha to meet up with the others. In the end she had been able to talk Alicia down from anything very frilly or poofy, but what she had was still a dress. A blue dress with some intricate designs, but otherwise fairly plain. Similarly, Alex had refused to let them go too crazy with makeup, just enough to not stand out at the party. There had been a lengthy discussion about whether Alex would be allowed to take her hair out of the ponytail she typically kept it in, but Alicia and Charlie caved eventually. All of it combined, the stupid dress stuff, the danger involved, the...socializing, it was all too much. Alex was legitimately *nervous*, and it showed on her face.

"Don't worry, Alex, you look great, and it's going to be fine," said Alicia.

Alex didn't really have a metric for if she did in fact look great. She had seen herself in the mirror, and she guessed it was okay, but she had no idea what to expect from this fancy party.

The meetup location was just outside the prince's chambers, where Darius, Isaac, and Anthony were talking.

Alicia got their attention. "Ahem, gentlemen; presenting Miss Alexandria Petrakis!" She gestured toward Alex with flourish and Charlie did the same.

Anthony and Isaac stared.

"Is that really her?" Isaac whispered, loud enough for Alex to hear, and she scowled.

"Okay, that's a yes," he said.

Anthony walked forward but he didn't take his eyes off Alex. "Alicia, what did you do to Alex?"

"Oh, Anthony, doesn't she look fantastic?"

"Well, I can tell *you* had fun dear," Anthony laughed.

Darius walked up to Alex who blushed and avoided eye contact.

Darius said, "You look great Alex."

That helped her a bit; Darius was always genuine. Not that looking good was Alex's goal.

The door to Calseous' room opened, and the prince walked out. He was dressed regally, although Alex had *expected* a crown.

He strode out of the doorway, eyes closed, smiling, and head held high.

He proclaimed, "How do I look?"

Everyone glanced at him briefly, but quickly turned back to Alex.

The prince opened his eyes and looked over at the group. He blushed, his eyes met Alex, and his jaw dropped.

That was a confidence boost, if she could make an actual prince, let alone this prince, blush, then she had truly beaten the girls in high school. It had only taken six years and a journey to a different world, but she'd take it.

"Miss Alex! I hardly recognize you!"

"Gee, thanks."

"I meant no offense. I daresay you clean up rather well!"

Alex sighed, "Yeah, that's still sort of insulting."

Calseous seemed to give up on complements and broke eye contact with Alex.

Darius quickly said, "We'll be watching from outside; you're not exactly prepped for a fight so don't hesitate to ask over the earpiece for backup."

"I wouldn't say I'm completely helpless," Alex smirked, slightly pulling up her dress to reveal her pistol strapped to her calf.

Charlie leaned over to Alicia, "Are you worried that we didn't notice her put that on?" Alicia nodded, and Alex laughed.

"Well," Calseous cleared his throat. "Shall we?" he offered Alex his arm.

Alex walked straight past him towards the party, "Not a chance."

CHAPTER 32

When they entered the ballroom, Alex was struck by two things—how loud it was, and the size of the peculiar room. It seemed to wrap all the way around the tower, with a couple of exits to outside terraces. At the center, once again, was the cylinder of the vertical aqueduct that carried the river water upwards.

The party had already started, and they were a bit late. The volume of the crowd was immediately unnerving to Alex.

About fifteen feet into the room, two women approached them. Their dresses were far more regal, and frilly than Alex's, and they wore matching colorful masks.

One woman said, "Calseous, we heard about the dreadful trip you had."

"Just dreadful," the other woman added.

"Yes well, Miss Alexandria here kept me quite safe," Calseous put on his most princely voice.

"Oh?" The first woman said, "A capable woman, how impressive!"

"Quite impressive," the second one added.

Alex just smiled and nodded, not sure how exactly to respond to any of that.

"She's a rather stoic one isn't she?" said the first.

"Rather stoic, indeed," the other added.

"Yes, well we have many folks to speak to, wonderful to see

you madams." Calseous dragged Alex away from the conversation. "What was that? You've completely frozen!"

With a forced smile Alex said, "There's a *lot* of people here, Calseous, and I know exactly *zero* of them. I am not the schmoozing type."

"Ah yes, Mister Isaac explained this term to me. Well, Miss Alex, I'm afraid you must schmooze as best you can, everything depends on it."

"No pressure..." Alex muttered.

"Now quickly, put this on," Calseous handed her the mask she had chosen earlier. She had gone for a rather simple blue one, to match her dress.

Calseous donned his own mask, when a booming voice said, "Prince Calseous, I see you're already hiding away in the corner."

"Councilor Aldron! What a pleasant surprise!" said Calseous.

Aldron looked squarely at Alex. "Indeed. I must say, your friend here made quite a scene at the court this morning."

Alex's smile was threatening to break, but she kept her cool. She wanted to snap back at him, but she needed to be polite.

"Yes, well, just keeping the discussion going."

"I meant to ask," Aldron began with narrowed eyes, "Why is it you speak so strangely? It's as if your words aren't your own."

Alex shot a glance at Calseous, blanking on how to explain *any* part of the technology that let her speak their language.

"It is a form of magic from her country, esteemed councilor," said Calseous, but he sounded nervous.

"I see, and what country is that?" The older man asked.

"Missouri," Alex blurted.

Calseous added, "Yes, Missouri, a *quite* far off land. Perhaps farther than any other known country."

"A bold claim to be sure, but one I'm inclined to believe. Do enjoy yourself, Calseous, you and your accompaniment," Aldron sneered and with drink in hand, he walked away.

Alex let the breath and tenseness escape through her mouth. "Oh my gosh that guy is such a…"

"I'm aware, Miss Alex, but let's keep our voices down shall we? The night is young and there are many unpleasant people to speak to," said Calseous.

"You make it sound so fun," Alex said sarcastically.

The next hour was full of uncomfortable conversation, silly masks, and political lobbying. As the night dragged on, Alex almost missed the suffering of trying on dresses with Alicia and Charlie. *Almost.* If she got one more comment on her rather plain dress, her way of speaking, or her *height*, she swore she would lose it.

As she listened to Calseous plead his case to a table of councilors, Alex was startled by a sudden, incredibly loud, trumpet.

"Attention please." A royal guard shouted from a balcony. She held up a scroll and began to read from it. "His majesty, King Arathos, has died. Taken by illness nought but ten minutes prior. Long live the kingdom." She ended in the standard salute.

A hush spread across the crowd, except for an occasional murmur or gasp. Calseous stood abruptly and began to walk away.

Alex followed closely behind. "Calseous, wait!" her whisper came out in a hiss.

Before she could stop him, he was blocked by two familiar faces.

Councilor Zalta said, "Calseous, I'm…so sorry. I cannot imagine."

Zalta's wife added, "If you need anything, please just reach out to us."

Calseous opened his mouth as though to respond but closed it. He trudged around them and out onto one of the terraces.

Zalta sighed and said to Alex, "This is not unexpected, the king has been ill for some time, but that does not take away from the pain he must be in."

"I appreciate it, councilor, but I have to go check on him," said

Alex. She started to go around the two before being stopped by a firm hand on her shoulder.

Zalta held her back, "Perhaps it is best that he is alone for now, to process things. I'm afraid we've our own matters to attend to. It was lovely to see you again, Miss Alex."

Alex waited for the couple to leave then she briskly went after Calseous. She found him sitting on a stone bench by the fountain in the center of the garden. He had removed his mask. She sat next to him and took off her own.

Calseous had tears in his eyes, but his expression was numb, Alex wasn't sure those tears would ever fall. She had no words for him, especially after the Zaltas had spoken such generic condolences to him.

After a brief pause, she gently put her hand on his shoulder. The silence in the air was almost serene allowing the sounds from the garden to prevail. As crickets chirped and leaves rustled, the light of the nearly full moon danced in the streams of water coming from the fountain.

In any other circumstance it would all be so beautiful, but at this moment it served only as a solemn backdrop to Calseous' own personal tragedy.

"I haven't spoken to my father in three months, Miss Alex. I knew this day would come, and so I did everything in my power to please him before he passed. To earn his respect, and the court's, I went on that terrible diplomatic journey, to prove I could be useful. I'm afraid that now I shall never know whether it was worth it."

Alex could feel his grief, and it made her heart ache.

She was unsure if she should ask her next question, but she wondered, "Were you close to your father, Calseous?"

"Perhaps, when I was quite young, but as I aged he grew more and more distant. Detached. After Mother vanished, we were truly strangers to one another. If I were to be truthful, I would say that Fraygor was the one who raised me after that."

Alex looked down, "He does seem pretty protective of you."

"Indeed, but I can see the way in which it weighs upon him. The responsibility, the constant worry. I fear I am nothing more than a burden, some bauble to be defended, but for no particular purpose. A useless adornment to a troubled kingdom."

Alex frowned. As hard as it was to see the court fling insults at him, this was even worse.

"Don't be so hard on yourself, based on what I've seen so far you're the only one even interested in fixing any problems."

Calseous didn't look up at her, "I do wish that I could believe that redeems my standing, but evidently that is not the case."

"What do you mean?"

"Look at the people around me, Miss Alex. Fraygor insists that I am constantly tended to, watched, and pandered like a child. Even when he leaves me for *more important matters* he leaves me with someone, such as yourself."

Alex couldn't disagree with this and let him continue.

"My father largely paid me no mind for the better part of ten years. My mother vanished without a trace. Much of the court finds me useless at best and detestable at worst."

"Calseous…"

"To think that I am surrounded by those devoted to me, and it feels as though not one of them truly *cares* for me. Am I truly that terrible? So, without value?" Now his eyes filled with tears.

Alex firmly said, "*Calseous.*"

For the first time he looked at her, and tears streamed down his cheeks.

"I…" Alex paused. "Calseous, *I* care."

He stared at her glumly, clearly doubtful.

"I *do,* and Fraygor does too, he's just terrible at showing it," Alex chuckled softly.

Calseous sniffed and chuckled with her. He looked back down at the floor.

"I'm serious though, Fraygor is protective *because* he cares. Maybe he's doing it the wrong way, maybe he needs to ease off a bit, but it's coming from a good place."

"I only wish that he could let me learn to, how would you put it, handle things myself?" Calseous said, "I do not think that it is possible to learn without being given the chance to do so. If I am always tended to, I will not ever learn. I am safe here in the capital, should I not be able to care for myself?"

Alex supposed that was true.

"Maybe you should just talk to him about it? I mean, you're right, you're probably a lot safer in the capital. Your enemies would need to be a lot more brazen to attack here. It's a less dangerous situation, so it's a good place to start being independent."

Calseous raised his head from its slumped position, "Perhaps, it would certainly be nice to have some room to breathe, to steal a phrase from Miss Alicia. I do grow tired of the constant tension, of fearing assassins lie around every corner."

"Yeah I would love it if that would stop happening, I think we've seen enough of those attempts on you for a lifetime," she tried to lighten the mood.

Calseous gave her a weak smile.

Alex took a deep breath, "Listen, I know that this is a really hard time in your life, and it sounds like there haven't been many easy parts, but we're going to work everything out. We *will* keep you safe, we *will* get me and my team home, and you *will* be king."

Calseous laughed, his somber smile spread across his face, "I daresay Miss Alex, how naively optimistic."

Maybe he was rubbing off on her, but she did really believe what she had said.

"I appreciate your encouragement, thank you Miss…Thank you *Alex*," Calseous said.

Alex nodded and took her hand off of his shoulder.

"Should we head back inside? If you're ready."

Calseous stood, "Actually, if it's alright, I would like to be alone for a time."

Alex hesitated, Fraygor's words ringing in her head, but she could see Calseous clearly had issues with people hovering over him. There hadn't been any danger since they got here, and if there was ever a time he needed to be alone, it was now, especially after the conversation they just had.

She nodded reluctantly, "Sure. Take all the time you need."

"I think I will head to the peak of the spire, when I was very young my father would take me there. It is a special place to me. Farewell Alex, do enjoy the party, if it does continue."

"Okay, Calseous, stay safe."

Alex watched him walk away, and she couldn't help but feel a tinge of pride. She had handled that pretty well, better than she was used to at least. She had mostly just been honest, spoken her mind, and maybe that was the real secret to those sorts of conversations.

CHAPTER 33

ALEX TOOK A MINUTE to recuperate outside. Even from the garden bench, she could hear the party. After taking a deep breath, she walked back inside.

Aluwain quickly approached her. "Alex, I've been looking for you. The party has been busy, and I've been preoccupied. Where is Prince Calseous?"

She could see the worry on Aluwain's face.

"He needed to be alone for a while," Alex said. "I'm assuming you heard the news about the king?"

Aluwain's expression soured, "Yes, that is why I've been looking for you two, to give my condolences."

"Well, like I said I think he needs to be alone for now, I'll go check on him in a little while."

Out of the corner of her eye she saw something familiar. Amidst the masked crowd, she caught glimpses of those same masks she had seen in Caltesia.

Suddenly a woman screamed, silencing the crowd.

At the edge of the gathering Alex could see Aldron doubled over, holding a hand to his side. One of the masked assassins stood over the councilor, a bloodied blade in his hand.

Alex hiked up her dress and grabbed her weapon.

"Aluwain, get down!" Alex fired her taser at the assassin. The masked figure didn't have time to react and dropped to the ground.

"Someone restrain him!" Alex ran up to Aldron and put a hand to her earpiece. "Charlie, get everyone in here right now!"

Broken glass crashed to the ground when the tower windows were smashed through. A half dozen more masked figures floated into the room, seeming to be propelled by that same purplish-blue energy Alex had seen before.

Chaos broke out and people ran from the ballroom as the assailants' fired blasts of their magic. As the room emptied, Alex saw only the assassins, and a handful of partygoers on the floor.

Her team ran into the room.

"Could use a little help here guys!" She ducked behind a pillar for cover, and her team joined her in firing shots at the masked assassins.

Two of the attackers caught rounds in their shoulders and were sent flying from the impact.

The magical shield barriers they had seen in Caltesia appeared once again blocking Alex and the others, but Darius moved around the side, to get past them.

The assassins grouped closely together and formed a tight circle with the barriers, still

taking fire from the team's pistols. Alex stopped shooting long enough to see that their opponents were grouped under one of the dangling chandeliers in the center of the room.

"Charlie!" she yelled, "Take out the chandelier!"

The red-haired woman quickly raised her rifle and took aim. With a loud crack, the chain holding the light fixture was severed, and it came crashing down on their enemies.

The barriers disappeared; the gunfire ceased. Alex breathed a sigh of relief and looked over at Aldron and the incapacitated assassin next to him. To her surprise she could see the killer's face, his mask was now missing.

She called Anthony over, and they hurried to the wounded

men. Anthony immediately applied medifoam to the councilor, who now lay completely prone on the floor.

The team gathered around her. "Good work, guys." Alex looked around for Aluwain, but she was nowhere to be found.

She must have fled with the rest of the crowd.

"We need to treat the wounded and make sure the attackers are knocked out. As soon as they're awake, we need answers."

She looked around at the aftermath of their brief skirmish when the doors to the ballroom burst open. Alex expected more attackers, but instead Fraygor and a whole contingent of royal guards rushed in.

Fraygor called, "Alex! What happened?"

"More of our masked friends," she gestured to the unconscious Aldron. "They seemed to be targeting some of the councilors."

Fraygor looked around frantically, "Where is Calseous?"

"After he heard the news about the King, he wanted to be alone."

Fraygor's expression turned to one of fury. "You left him *alone?!*" His shouting drew the attention of everyone nearby.

Alex defended her decision. "He needed space. We talked about it, but he needs to process some things. Besides, if he had been here, he would have been a target too."

Fraygor scowled at her, "You fool! How could you be so careless."

Alex returned his scowl with one of her own and she raised her voice, "Fool? You're the one who dumped him on me. Fraygor, you don't have to baby him. He said he feels like all he's good for is being protected!"

"He can't be left alone. I won't allow it," Fraygor said.

"Why? I get that it's your duty or whatever, but why do you take it so personally? Enough to yell at me like this!" Alex waved an arm to emphasize her point.

"Because…"

"Because *what?*" she shouted.

"Because he's my son!" Fraygor shouted, his voice echoed across the entire room. The echo gradually faded, and Alex stood in shock.

In the silence she tried to process Fraygor's statement.

"Your…son?" It was almost a whisper.

"Yes," Fraygor stared directly at her, "I am Calseous' father. Not the king."

The royal guards on either side of him seemed just as stunned, and each briefly glanced at Fraygor, then at each other.

Fraygor said softly, "I was the queen's protector. We fell in love, and she bore Calseous. We feared the worst for her if word got out, and so he was claimed as the king's own blood."

Alex still stared at him.

"Your…lady love. Far away," Alex smiled.

"Yes," Fraygor said, "Queen Menara."

Alicia and Charlie stood awkwardly to the side; they seemed uncomfortable hearing this conversation.

Anthony continued working on Aldron, but it appeared he heard everything, too.

"Alex, I can explain this further later," Fraygor began, "but right now I need to make sure he's safe."

Alex sighed, releasing some of the tension, "He said he was going to the tip of the spire."

Fraygor turned around and started to depart, but he looked back at Alex. "Thank you. I'm…sorry for the way I treated you." he briskly walked away.

Charlie sidled up next to Alex, "Well, I didn't see that one coming."

"I should go with him," Alex said, "You guys got things covered here?"

"Go, boss," said Anthony, "We've got it."

Alex smiled. That was the first time Anthony had called her 'boss'.

She left her team to their work, exited the room, and was stopped by a crowd of partygoers. She heard many thanks, a great deal of crying, but she heard her name being called above everything else. The two women from the start of the party were flagging her down.

"Miss Petrakis!" one said, running up to her.

"Yes?" Alex stopped but was impatient.

"We've spoken to some of the other councilors, after this development I do not think you will find any opposition to the investigation, and you shall have your access to the archives as well." the woman proclaimed, loud enough for everyone to hear.

A small cheer erupted from the crowd, and more thanks followed. Alex felt awkward. *They sure changed their opinions fast.*

"Thanks. I'm sorry, but I need to go quickly. I have to check on the prince," she pushed through the crowd.

Once clear of the mass of people, she started running up the stairs. She knew the elevators would be faster, but she had no clue which ones to take. All stairs had to lead up though, right? As she ascended one set, the interior of the tower shifted to the dark stone of Aluwain's floor. She walked past Aluwain's study but doubled back to check on the mage.

"Oh, Alex!" said Aluwain.

"Aluwain, are you alright? I lost track of you in all the chaos."

"Oh, I ran the second I saw danger. I'm not one for combat."

Alex smiled. She supposed that was fair, Aluwain did seem the delicate type.

"We're getting our archive access now, so there's that at least. I have to go make sure Calseous is okay."

Aluwain was pouring over documents and tomes and took a moment to respond.

"Oh yes, that's delightful," she didn't take her eyes off her work.

Alex raised an eyebrow. "Is everything okay? You seem distracted."

Aluwain didn't respond, but she frowned.

Alex walked over and tried to look at whatever held Aluwain's attention. But she hurriedly gathered the spread papers.

"Oh Alex, this is personal. I'm sorry, but you can't see it!" Aluwain panicked, and accidentally knocked a stack of books off her desk.

Another object fell too, and Skidded across the floor, Alex saw it. She couldn't be certain, the room was dimly lit, but as she picked it up her suspicions were confirmed.

In her hand she held one of the smooth ivory white masks the assassins wore.

"Aluwain I…" Pain coursed through her body. She couldn't move, she could barely breathe, but she saw Aluwain; the young mage, holding her staff, and channeling a dark green energy toward Alex.

"I really wish you had not seen that, Alex."

"Why?" Alex strained to speak a single word, "The mask…"

Aluwain looked Alex directly in the eyes. "An old tradition of the Zalta clan, my ancestors. Long since lost to time, until now."

Alex struggled. She still had her weapon drawn from the fight but couldn't move a muscle to raise it. Her hand spasmed as she tried to move it, and one of her fingers squeezed the trigger for her taser. The prongs shot into the ground and crackled with electricity.

To Alex's surprise, the electricity from the taser shot reacted with the magic holding her in place. As energy arced through the magic Aluwain was channeling, it glowed brighter and brighter.

With a flash and a crash, Aluwain's staff flew from her hands as her spell exploded in front of her. Both women were sent flying, but Alex was able to get to her feet before Aluwain. Raising her weapon, she pointed it squarely at the young mage.

"You snake!" Alex yelled. "You've been in on this the whole time? Helping to kill Calseous? Some friend you are!"

Aluwain sat against the wall, "I…I didn't know for sure until now."

Alex furrowed her brow, "What do you mean?"

"My father would tell me stories of our family's past. When I saw the masks…I needed to be sure. Alex you must understand, I didn't know!"

Alex lowered her weapon slightly, "Why did you attack me then?"

Aluwain winced in pain as she stood, "I am sorry, I panicked, I don't know how to process what I now know. My father is a killer," Aluwain barely got the words out. "But I want no part in his schemes. I would never hurt Calseous!"

Alex cautiously lowered her weapon, "We'll talk about this later, but I need you to show me the way to the top of the spire. I need to make sure Calseous is safe."

Aluwain's eyes shot wide open, "The spire top? No no no, my father was headed there last I saw him!"

Alex's blood ran cold. "Come on!" She reached for her earpiece as she sprinted out of the room, "Charlie, I need you guys at the top of the tower ASAP."

CHAPTER 34

ALEX BURST THROUGH THE DOOR to the peak of the tower. "Calseous!"

Rain poured down, the ground slick as thunder crashed above them.

Zalta stood at the top of a wide set of stairs, framed by the flashes of lightning. Fraygor ran at the councilor, sword in hand, as he narrowly avoided a ball of fire.

Alex scoffed, "Oh great, your dad is magic too?"

Aluwain sheepishly nodded.

Alex looked around for Calseous. He was behind Fraygor lying on the ground, barely holding himself up on one arm.

Alex charged Zalta but was pushed back by a blast of invisible energy when he pointed his open palm at her.

Zalta yelled, "Back, you! You've gotten in the way for long enough."

"Father!" Aluwain said, "Stop! This is madness!"

Zalta locked Fraygor in place with the green magic and glared at his daughter. "Madness? This is our birthright!" Zalta tossed Fraygor aside; he rolled down the stairs landing in a heap near Alex.

Alex got back on her feet and fired a shot directly at Zalta, who now stood over the Prince. Instead of blocking it as the other mages had, he raised a hand and suspended the bullet in the air. It rotated back towards Alex, and she had only a split second to roll out of the way before her own projectile came back at her.

"Aluwain, destroy these fools!" Zalta commanded. "For generations our family has sat by as this wretched kingdom imposed its will on us. Now is our chance, we can take back what is rightfully ours!"

Aluwain clutched her staff, tears spilling down her cheeks, "Father, what are you talking about?"

Her team arrived from the entrance as Alex tried to help Fraygor up.

"It's Zalta!" she shouted.

Zalta pushed Alex and Fraygor towards the rest of the team.

"Who do you think settled these lands?" Zalta boomed. "Our people have lived here longer than any others, and yet we have been subjugated by one nation or another for over a thousand years!"

Finally getting Fraygor up, Alex passed him off to Alicia, "I need you to make sure he's okay. We need to get to the prince."

"What's the plan? I don't see any chandeliers this time around," said Charlie.

"He's been tossing me and Fraygor around like we're punching bags. We have to rush him together." Alex didn't take her eyes off of the prince.

"Anthony, try to flank around, get the prince treatment as soon as you can. Everyone else, distract Zalta and keep him on his toes."

Charlie said, "I mean, he's been monologuing this whole time. I think he's distracting himself just fine."

With a series of nods, the team moved into action. Isaac on one side, Darius on the other, and Charlie lay back, firing her powerful rifle.

Zalta opened a magic barrier, far larger than those the other mages had used.

Zalta fired a blast at Isaac.

"These other-worlders have been a nuisance for far too…" he sent Darius flying backwards, "LONG!" He shouted, sending a bolt of lightning from his hand; it landed on Charlie's rifle. The weapon and its ammunition detonated, and Charlie was knocked to the ground.

"My baby!" she cried.

Zalta said, "Aluwain! Don't you see? The magic our clan has honed for generations places us above the common people. These fools and their trinkets are no match for a true mage!"

Alex was running towards Aluwain, but the younger woman was already climbing up the stairs.

"Father please!" she pleaded as she approached him, "This must end!"

Zalta scowled at her, "If you will not honor our ancestors as I do, then you are *in the way.*"

Aluwain grabbed at Zalta's robes, tears still streaming down her face. "Please!" Zalta struggled with his daughter for control of her staff.

"You, foolish, naive girl!" he bellowed. Alex stood at the bottom of the stairs, trying to get a line of sight on Zalta to take a shot but she was worried she would hit Aluwain.

In the struggle for the staff, the crystal on the tip started to glow.

Zalta shouted and wrenched the staff from Aluwain's hands. In the process, the crystal tip sliced Aluwain's side.

She tumbled down the stairs, slid across the slick ground, and crashed at the bottom.

Zalta grinned as he held the staff in his hand, "I sent my daughter to the archives to find us ancient magic we could use to deal with this pitiful prince and the other factions vying for power."

Aluwain lay on the ground, barely breathing.

He gestured to the tip of the staff. "When she returned with this crystal, she told me it could open doors to another world. I thought nothing of it, I want to rule *this* land, nothing more."

He raised the staff, and the crystal glowed; loose flowing energy spilled out of it.

"My foolish daughter experimented with it and inadvertently got you involved."

As the magic flowed from the staff, it crackled with energy and began forming a circle.

Alex was met with a familiar sight. A tear in the air, in reality, a *Rift*.

"Go home Miss Petrakis. You are not wanted here," Zalta said.

Alex's eyes misted when she looked at the Rift.

Inside she could see a field of wheat, hay-bales, and a tractor. Beyond that, a city, a modern *Earth* city.

All this time away from home, all this time stranded in this strange land, and there it was. An easy escape. She looked around at her teammates, then at Aluwain.

Zalta yelled, "Take your wretched minions with you and be gone!"

Alex's eyes locked onto Calseous, who even as he lay bleeding on the ground, met her gaze.

The temptation to run through the Rift was still there, but it was overwhelmed by another familiar emotion—duty.

Alex glared at Zalta, "They're not my minions. They're my *people*. And you still have one of them."

With rage in her heart Alex charged at Zalta. She climbed the stairs as fast as she could but tucked to the left to avoid a bolt of fire from the mage.

Alex lunged at him and grabbed the staff.

Zalta had a crazed look in his eyes. "If you insist on staying a thorn in my side, then you will perish!" he boomed.

He growled and shoved Alex down the stairs and let go of the staff in the process.

Alex joined Aluwain at the bottom.

"Alex!" Anthony called. He knelt over Aluwain, treating her wound.

He motioned to Aluwain's arm. "I have no idea what's happening."

Through Aluwain's fair skin, Alex could see a purplish-blue energy flowing through her veins and emanating from her cut.

Alex tore a large strip off of her dress and handed it to Anthony.

"Here, use this. I have bigger issues right now," she turned back to Zalta.

Darius and Isaac still fired at Zalta keeping him occupied. Alex racked her brain trying to form a plan. This guy was on a whole other level than anything they had dealt with before, and she had no idea how to counter magic.

She looked down at her gun and then to Aluwain and the strange effect the crystal had on her. Then it clicked and she leapt into action.

"Darius! Isaac, tasers!"

Both men prepped and fired the stun-guns at Zalta's shield, disrupting it just as they had done to Aluwain's magic earlier.

Small gaps formed in the center of the barrier. Alex pulled the prongs out of her own stun-gun, and forcefully jabbed them into Aluwain's staff.

Please let this work.

Alex stood, and with a hefty throw, launched the staff at Zalta as though it were a javelin. The staff sailed through a gap in the barrier and implanted itself in Zalta's chest. The wind knocked out of him, he stepped backwards, and his barrier dissipated. The purplish-blue energy spread throughout his body at a far faster pace than it had Aluwain's. From the center outwards his skin began to flake and crumble.

"Hit him!" Alex shouted.

Darius, Isaac, and Alex each fired a volley of shots at the mage, the impacts knocking him even closer to the edge of the tower.

Alex pulled the trigger on her weapon and sent electricity coursing through the taser wires all the way up into the staff.

The crystal, still embedded in Zalta's chest, glowed, the intense light showing even through his skin. Suddenly, his entire body glowed, the crystal's light becoming almost blinding. With a deep boom, the staff shattered, and the crystal surged with energy.

With an otherworldly scream, Zalta was sent flying off the ledge. The crystal finally burst, shattering inside of him, and turning the mage's entire body to dust in an instant.

CHAPTER 35

ALEX WATCHED as their former enemy blew away in the wind, and the Rift snapped shut. She dwelled on it for a moment, but their work wasn't done. "Anthony?"

Anthony stood over Aluwain, "It was risky, but I think it worked."

The discoloration on the young mage's skin had stopped at the elbow but had clearly traveled in her veins throughout her body. The strip from Alex's dress was tightly tied around her arm.

"How did you stop it?"

Anthony held up a syringe of medifoam. "Miracles of modern medicine. I injected it directly into her bloodstream. She'll be knocked out for a good while. But it seems to have worked," he said with a smile.

Alex was relieved after seeing Aluwain struggle with her father. There was no doubt in Alex's mind that Aluwain was innocent. She had been used by Zalta, just as much a victim as Calseous.

"Anthony, if she's stable, I need you to come with me."

Just then, Alicia and Charlie approached, assisting Fraygor, his arms around their shoulders.

"He only just woke up," said Alicia.

Fraygor, his face groggy and his eyes heavy, looked up to see Calseous at the top of the stairs.

"Calseous!" he broke free of the two women's grip, and he

limped desperately up the steps.

"Anthony, come on," Alex followed him.

When they reached Calseous, he was on his back, his eyes barely open.

Anthony began checking his wounds.

"Calseous, I'm here," Fraygor kneeled next to the prince.

Calseous coughed, "Fraygor it…seems you were right; I should never stray far from you. I'm sorry, it would seem that you will not see me become king,"

Anthony said quietly, "Alex, it's a deep stab wound. We found a poison just like this on the councilors in the ballroom. The medi-foam won't work on this one."

The rest of the team gathered at the top of the stairs, all eyes on the prince. Unphased by the attention, Calseous kept his eyes locked on his guard.

"Fraygor, my friend. You have been more of a father to me than the king ever could be, and for that I am grateful."

Fraygor's eyes filled with tears, something Alex never thought she'd see.

"Calseous, I *am* your father. We are blood, the queen…your mother is alive and well. I love her, and I love *you,"* Fraygor tried to hold back the tears.

In his weakened condition, Calseous looked confused. Finally, a smile crossed his lips, "Then it would seem I can die happy, knowing that I was more than an assignment to you."

Calseous looked at Alex and tears welled up in her eyes. She knelt next to him, her dress soaked and tattered.

"Miss…Alex. Just Alex. Our journey has brought me more excitement than anything in my life, perhaps a bit too much," he struggled when a chuckle escaped his throat. "These past weeks, I feel as though I can now say I have truly *lived*. I am sorry to end it so abruptly. I would have very much enjoyed continuing our adventures."

Alex's tears flowed, "Don't apologize you idiot! You're going to be fine; we'll figure something out, we always do."

Alex wasn't sure she believed her own words, but she felt the need to speak them nonetheless.

Anthony said, "Alex, I can't do anything for him. Even if I sealed the wound, the poison would still kill him."

"It's not a mundane poison."

Everyone turned to see Aluwain standing behind them, and despite their apparent shock, she continued.

"It's a magical poison. So, it reacts to magic. The Zalta clan used it to poison enemies by sharing the same drink and then giving themselves the magical *'antidote'* so to speak. Quite clever," she approached Calseous.

"How are you awake?" asked Anthony.

"I'm not sure," Aluwain put her hand to the prince's wound. "But I feel different, I suppose that's best saved for later."

As Aluwain channeled her magic, her eyes glowed purple, and a light blue glow spread over Calseous' wound. The prince gasped, the color returned to his face, and his wound sealed.

Anthony held two fingers to the prince's wrist, "He's stable, how on Earth?"

"How on *Vertos!*" Aluwain corrected proudly, "And I daresay Anthony, the miracles of modern magic!"

Calseous sat up, his arms barely supporting him, "Ah, well that was quite unpleasant."

Alex was ready to scold him for his nonchalant response to his revival. But before she could say a word, Fraygor lunged forward with a hug.

"My son!"

Calseous returned the hug, his arms still weak, "My father!" he said, and he wept.

Everyone else smiled and Alex stood, pretending she had not cried at all.

"Well, good work team. Let's…" Alex remembered the crystal, and what Zalta had said about it, "...actually, I'm not sure what to do at this point."

Aluwain stood beside Alex, "The crystal was the only thing in the archives I ever found related to the Rift, I must apologize for lying about having access to them.

Alex looked at the spot where the Rift had been, and her heart sank. She turned to Aluwain, "I don't suppose you have any ideas?"

Aluwain looked at her arm, now a dark purple, "Something has changed in me, the magic of the crystal, it seems to be affecting my natural magic potential."

Alex had no clue what that meant.

"Oh yes, you see some people *learn* to use magic, and some are born with a natural potential magical energy within them," explained Aluwain. "I believe that whatever magic the Rift crystal held, a small part of it has now been implanted in my own."

Alex's eyes widened. In fact, the whole team's eyes widened, "You mean… you can open a Rift?"

"Perhaps with enough practice, yes," Aluwain narrowed her eyes as she held her hands close together, focusing on the energy between them. As she strained, that same crackle of energy formed between her palms and a small Rift opened in her grasp.

"Oh great, now we can send an apple through," Charlie chided at the unimpressive size of the Rift.

Aluwain struggled to maintain it, but eventually her effort gave out, and the Rift closed. Exhausted, she huffed, "Like I said, practice will be needed."

Alex said, "It's better odds than we had before. Thank you, Aluwain."

Alex noticed Fraygor clutching Calseous, tears still streaming. Alicia was also crying which seemed natural for her. Weeping, Charlie held the scorched remains of her rifle.

Isaac approached her.

"It's uh- It's okay, Charlie. You can build a new one."

Charlie sniffed, "Y-yeah! I'll build a better one, and *bigger* too," she said through her tears.

Alex looked at all of them. "I think we've had enough excitement for one evening, guys. Now what?"

Darius grinned, "There's still a ton of food down in the ballroom kitchen! I'm starving."

Isaac's eyes lit up, "Is that a challenge, Darius?"

"It is now!"

The two men walked down the stairs; the trash talk already starting.

"Actually," the prince said, "I would rather like some dinner."

"Me too," said Alex.

Anthony and Fraygor helped Calseous walk down the stairs. Everyone but Alex followed them.

They had made it through the fight of their lives.

"Alex!" Alicia called, "Aren't you coming?"

"Yep. But first," Alex said, "I'm getting out of this ridiculous dress."

CHAPTER 36

IT HAD BEEN A WEEK since their fight with Zalta. Everyone had recuperated and they were preparing to board the ferry. The plan was to head back to the outpost where the first Rift had closed, and *hopefully* be able to get one to open.

Aluwain had been shut away in her study with Isaac and Alicia, practicing and training her newfound powers. She was confident she could open a stable Rift now, but Alex would believe it when she saw it.

About to board the ferry, Alex heard a crackle over the long-range radio for the first time in a while. Stepping away towards the river, she spoke into it, "Pyetro?"

"*There you are, Alex. We've been trying to contact you for ages!*" the Ukrainian man's voice chimed through the radio.

"Yeah, we kinda went through some mountains. Is something wrong?"

"*Oh no, something is very, very right my friend!*" Pyetro said excitedly. Alex could see his smile even over the radio.

"Yeah? What's the good news?"

"*Oh, Alex, I can't just tell you. Excitement, my American friend, is all in the presentation,*" Pyetro's voice came through clearer and clearer.

Alex was curious as to what he was on about, but her train of thought was interrupted when she heard a very familiar sound approaching from the distance.

There's no way.

The hum of engines thundered overhead as an aircraft, an *Earth* aircraft, passed low over them.

"Pyetro is that?"

"Yes, one of your American MC-32 Albatross. It was the last thing to be sent through the Rift before it closed," Pyetro said. *"It was all in pieces, so we've spent the whole time you were gone assembling it. And the best part?"*

Alex watched as the plane turned back towards them and rapidly slowed.

"It's amphibious!" Pyetro proclaimed.

The plane landed on the river with a spray of water, coming to a stop downstream.

"It's remotely operated, but we sent it up so that we could use it as a relay to get a radio signal to you." Pyetro said, *"I trust you can fly it home?"*

Alex said over the radio, "I would love nothing more."

The team carried their gear to the floating aircraft. The buggies wouldn't fit on the plane, so they would have to be left behind.

Alex watched as the wheels of the plane lowered and it rolled out of the water and onto the river shore. Everyone piled in, although it took some convincing to assure Aluwain it was safe.

Alex piloted the aircraft back down into the water, turned downstream and shoved the throttle forward. With a mighty drum of its engines the aircraft lifted into the air after just a short distance. Calseous walked up to the cabin, sitting on a chair behind Alex.

"This is quite the machine. I daresay your airships are even better than ours!" he said.

"It's an air*plane*," Alex said, "But yeah, it's pretty amazing. They used to use this model back when I was in the air force to rescue downed pilots in the ocean."

Calseous squinted, "I haven't the faintest clue what most of that means, but it is fascinating nonetheless."

Alex smiled. Maybe it was her turn to explain a bit of Earth to him. Fully in her element, the rest of the trip Alex rattled off all of her knowledge about this specific aircraft.

As Alex lowered their altitude to land, Calseous said, "You truly do seem to enjoy flying."

"It's one of my great loves."

The radio, now much clearer, transmitted Pyetro's voice. "*There is a short strip you can use to land.*"

Sure enough, Alex looked out to see a makeshift dirt runway off to their left.

"You guys have been busy." Alex said over the radio.

"What did you expect us to do?" Pyetro said with a laugh, *"You thought we would, how do you say it, 'twiddle our thumbs?'"*

Alex smirked as she lined up and landed them smoothly on the ground. The entire camp had come out to greet them, and as the team unloaded, Alex got an immediate hug from Pyetro. The team exchanged handshakes with the people from the outpost, and Darius in particular got a few hugs.

With shaky legs, Aluwain stepped out of the plane.

Alex walked her to the center of camp.

"Okay, Aluwain, moment of truth."

With all eyes on her, Aluwain raised her hands to the empty space where the first Rift had been. As she strained, a spark of electricity formed in the air, the tear appeared and grew wider and wider.

On the other side they could see the mountain base, and about a dozen stunned scientists. Cheers rang out across the camp.

Alex quickly ran through the Rift, which now had no gap between the two sides. "We need you to power up the reactors!"

Hours later, the other side sent across a hefty portable generator.

Alex asked as she looked at Isaac and Alicia. "Are you guys sure about this theory?"

"Well, Alicia knows the specifics. It was just a random idea I had," said Isaac.

"If we pump electricity from *both* ends of the rift, it may stabilize it. Aluwain thinks that there is a polarity to the rifts, and that if energy flows from both sides, it will balance the magic," explained Alicia.

Aluwain stood behind Alicia sheepishly. She sighed, "It's only a theory."

Alex nodded and gave a signal to Pyetro who quickly powered up the generator. As electricity flowed from a tesla coil on the generator, the rift began to suck it up and change in shape. Gone were the jagged edges and shards, instead a perfect square formed in the air, settling neatly on the ground.

Alicia hugged Alex and she watched all around her as cheers erupted from both ends of the Rift. They had done it; they could go home.

In the days following, they moved back and forth between the Rift. The outpost began to expand rapidly. While they had been on their journey, the people in Kairnos' village had become close friends with those of the outpost. As their base grew in this world, so did that bond. Within weeks, the outpost was more like a town, and vendors from the village would come and sell their wares there, everyone from Earth hungry for otherworldly goods and souvenirs.

Alex, alongside Darius, stood in front of Norgaard, the commander of the Looking Glass base.

"You're telling me that after being trapped in another world for over a month your first instinct is to go *back?*"

"Your first orders were exploration. There's a whole world over there, and it's a *lot* more complicated than we thought," explained Alex.

"We think if we can establish connections with the various nations, that exploration will go a lot smoother," Darius added.

Norgaard sighed, "What exactly is it you're asking for then?"

Alex and Darius shared a glance before Alex spoke. "A blank check, sir. Let us be the away team again. Let us explore this world and be the first contact. We know it better than anyone else. You can't argue with that."

Norgaard looked down at the dozen reports he had read over the past week.

"I suppose I can't. Very well, do as you see fit. We'll be here to support you," Alex walked back through the Rift and into the bustling outpost, Darius turned to her and asked,

"What's next boss? Where are we headed first?"

"I have one idea."

Days later, the team was loading up the plane once again.

"Fraygor, did you finish those directions?" Alicia asked.

Fraygor handed her a map. They hadn't seen him *or* Calseous in over a week, they had been back at the capital.

Calseous was now officially the king. Zalta's assassinations at the party had been directed at all of his own rivals, each of which were *also* trying to kill the prince. An investigation by the council led to several other arrests, and soon enough the votes turned in Calseous' favor.

Now however, he loaded onto the plane with the rest of them. Not dressed in regal garb, but adventuring gear like everyone else.

Calseous and Fraygor sat down inside the plane. "Are you looking forward to seeing your mother?" Fraygor asked.

"She hasn't seen me in over a decade, what will I even say?"

Fraygor smiled, "Your mother didn't go a day without speaking of you, anything you say will delight her."

Alex stepped onto the plane. "You guys ready? It's a long flight. You said the country was Galos, right?"

Fraygor nodded, "Indeed. A month away by cart, far in the east."

Alex walked to the cockpit, "I think we can cut that a lot shorter."

She sat down in the pilot's seat and looked back into the cabin to see her whole team, including Calseous and Fraygor.

She grinned, "Is everyone ready?"

Charlie polished her new rifle, "Yep!"

Everyone else just nodded.

Alex turned back to the runway ahead of her. She slowly eased the throttle forward.

"Our orders were to explore," she proclaimed as they lifted off the ground. "So, let's get exploring!"

THE END

www.ingramcontent.com/pod-product-compliance
Lightning Source LLC
Chambersburg PA
CBHW020322030826
48979CB00022B/790
* 9 7 9 8 8 9 4 5 4 0 0 1 6 *